Washed in the Blood

A novel by Roger Pinckney

EVENING POST BOOKS
Our Accent Is Southern!

© 2021 Roger Pinckney

All rights reserved. No part of this book may be reproduced or transmitted in any form or by any means, electronic or mechanical, including photocopying, recording, or by any information storage and retrieval system, without permission in writing from the copyright owner.

Pinckney, Roger. Washed in the Blood
Published by Evening Post Books, Charleston, South Carolina.

ISBN-13: 978-1-929647-59-0

Cover and interior design by Michael J. Nolan

Dedication

For the ladies, the many who caught my eye, the few who touched my heart. You know who you are.

Chapter One

The Gospel According to Mullet

Deep down in October, Rut and Meatball Jenkins and Meatball's cousin Jimmie Jenkins sat on the end of the dock, waiting on the last of the crabbers, chewing on that old Gospel pie.

Meatball was the three-hundred-pound ice, diesel and gas man at Spanky Lufkin's seafood dock on Lucy Point Creek. Palmetto log piling, sun-warped pine decking, tin-roof, rattle-window office at the end, it leaned this way and that, according to the last hurricane wind.

Meatball weighed the shrimp and crabs, wrote the chits and Mr. Spanky deducted the ice, bait and fuel, and cut checks every Friday afternoon. The Stop-and-Rob bacon, bologna and Wonder Bread grocery store and the Stop-and-Rob liquor store were both up on Sam's Point Road, not far away. A man could live pretty good if he laid back some of his catch.

Meatball was also a deacon in the Friendship Baptist Church, over on Coosaw Island, where you come to Jesus every Sunday even if you already come the week before, so you dare not question his measure. He spoke pure Gullah, the Geechee creole the roots of which arrived on the slave ships four hundred years ago. Written like it sounds, you could not read it. If you heard him speak, you'd wish he came with subtitles.

Meatball eyed the tide and expounded upon the Book of Exodus, a favorite about the Hebrew flight from slavery in Egypt-land.

"Them chillren been bunch up on the beach and the Pharaoh was a'comin hard, them chariot wheels jus' a strikin' fire, like the East Coast *Champeen* train coming shrew Yemasee. Them chillren got no place for to run, no place for to hide."

Tide was dropping, dropping, almost dead low now. The wind mumbled and whispered off to nothing and the gnats set to gnawing — each 'bout as big as the finest pepper grain, Lord knows how a thing so small can hurt so bad.

A long-legged "pojo," which is a great blue heron, high stepped it to the edge of the creek, eyed a school of mud minnows swirling in the low-tide shallows. Saturday night strutters at the Huck and Buck Community Center Juke Joint, where the straight razors flew high, wide and frequent, learned their best moves from a pojo.

"Then Moses he lif' up he rod an' they come up a mighty wind."

"We needs a bit of breeze right now," Jimmie twitched and swatted. "These ting tear me up."

Down here, they have what's called "the salute," waving bugs off their faces, the table grace, waving them off their food. Rut fired a cigarette.

It helped.

"You know that bad blow back in '59?" Meatball asked.

Jimmie was just a baby but Rut and Meatball remembered. "Blowed low tide clean up to high."

That would be Hurricane Gracie, 160 mph in gusts. They named all the hurricanes after women in those days, and Rut never figured why anybody who knew anything about women would want it any other way.

"You know Moses, he a bad man. He have terrible temperament. He kilt a 'gyptian."

"Cut 'em or he shoot 'em?" Jimmie wanted to know.

"I ain' know that, but I know he kill 'em sho-nuff dead …"

A catspaw of wind ghosted up river and they were glad to get it.

"… The wind she blowed so bad, the water she roll back an' Moses an' de chillren walk cross the sea wif dry shoe …"

Jimmie considered his brogans, military surplus with slits cut across the toes to ease his bunions. He wore no socks.

"… But ol' Pharaoh he still a'comin' so dey hotfoot it, and 'bout halfway cross, Moses trip on a mullet and he cuss and kick that fush … cuss 'em an kick 'em so hard, both dem mullet eye swap round to one side, an' he be the very fust flounder."

"A flounder got all-both he eyeballs on one side and he mouf up front. How he eat?"

"He eat mighty good," Meatball said. "You knows that."

Rut lit another smoke.

Christmas Eve, Lucy Point Creek. No moon but the stars were so bright they threw shadows; so close, it looked like you could reach up and pluck them right out of the sky; so quiet, you could hear the ocean breathe.

All across these islands the faithful were gathered in their waiting rituals, singing up midnight and the day the Savior was born. Way off through the pines and oaks and mournful Spanish moss, way up in the middle of the Coosaw high-ground at Friendship Baptist, the boys could hear them sing.

Go down Moses, way down in Egypt-land

Go down, tell that Pharaoh, let my people go …

Rut and Yancey set out in a skiff. They reckoned it was OK, as Jesus chose his first disciples from among fishermen, even though neither could name them with any certainty.

Moses was set adrift as an infant in a wattle and pitch basket upon the Nile — crocodile bait. But Pharaoh's little daughter went down to the water to bathe in the cool of the day and there she saw the basket. And she looked inside and called him her own, her beautiful son.

Hard to get shut of Moses, specially 'round the water. Indeed, they'd borrowed the boat from Moses Simmons: a fourteen-footer, cypress sides, oak bow-spit and transom with a half-inch plywood bottom, light and nimble. Put your back to the oars, she'd throw a wake. But they were just easing along on the last of the ebb of seabound water.

Israel was in Egypt-land
  Let my people go!

Oppressed so hard they could not stand
  Let my people go!

Too small for an oyster bateau, Moses used her for casting for shrimp, but the boys were gigging flounder this time. Summertime, the water looks like thin pea soup, but when the temperature gets down to 50 degrees, the plankton and diatoms and what-all die back, then you can see eight, ten feet easy, sometimes more. "How much water we got, Yance?"

"Eighteen-and-a-half feet."

"How the hell you know that?"

"Cause I can see eighteen and can't see no bottom."

A lamp hung low over the bow on a five-foot piece of two-by-two. It was an old-time incandescent streetlamp, complete with shade so it would light up the bottom and not the fishermen's eyes. It was supposed to run on house current, but out there in the skiff, they used a six-volt tractor battery instead. It worked but threw an uncertain, yellow, quavering light.

Rut leaned on the oars, headed for shallow water. "Lem'me know when you see bottom."

Yancey peered over the light, snapped his fingers when he saw it and they swung down-tide, perfect.

Yancey had a three-prong gig, like what you'd use to stab a bullfrog but bigger — five, six tines or so — on the end of a ten-foot bamboo pole. Standing there on the bow of that old skiff, he looked sorta like Neptune, or maybe Poseidon, but he was younger and it was wintertime so he had on more clothes.

Rut kept to the oars, quiet as he could. They had wrapped them in gunnysacks, tied with sisal baling twine to muffle the rock-rock noise of the oarlocks. Gotta sneak up on flounder — with both eyes looking up. Flounder got no ears but can hear a frog fart with a thin line of nerves down their back. You can see it plain once you scrape the scales off.

Yancey kept the gig point below the water — no splash when he made his move.

First fish, two pounds. Second fish, size of a dump-truck mud flap. Yancey peeled each off the gig with his foot, flipped them bleeding and flopping into a galvanized washtub that had two inches of fresh cut spartina cane in the bottom to damp the rattle.

A few more strokes on the oars and Yancey cussed. "Damn thing took off for deep water. Missed him clean."

Gone in a blink, leaving a little mud trail like a stream of brown smoke. Mullet and spottail bass will do the same, ditto sea trout if you're lucky enough to find them. "Want me to call up a porpoise?"

They called them porpoises. Yankees call them dolphins. Confusing. The porpoise is a mammal, and there is another dolphin, a deep-water pelagic fish. Yankee children would break down and cry in seafood restaurants 'cause they thought they were eating Flipper. That's why it says "mahi" on menus now.

The porpoise is about the closest thing to a dog, but smarter. They follow people and love people and even though they don't need people, they will come when you call. Rut took an oar and thumped on the bottom of the boat — *bump, bump, bump*. Wasn't long before they heard a throaty *whump* of a porpoise blowing somewhere out in the dark. That thing knew the drill.

It swung in alongside and followed as all the fish crowded the mudbank trying to stay clear. And there Yancey was waiting with his gig. If he missed, or if he spooked a fish, the porpoise would nab it. But he didn't miss. Three more flounder came aboard quick as it took to tell you.

But Great God-a-Mighty, the fat-back mullet behind them! The porpoise had them hemmed tight against the bank, three pounds each, fin to fin. Too many to count; more fish than water.

Rut was not saved, not yet anyway, but he knew his Bible stories from Sunday school. The disciples were out fishing and weren't catching much. Then somebody came strolling along the bank and hollered, "Throw your net on the other side of the boat!"

It was Jesus, but too far away for the disciples to see who He was. "Who that fool telling us how to fish?"

"Throw your net on the other side of the boat!"

And so they did, and the net got so full of fish, yea, they tore it asunder trying to get it back aboard. *Tore asunder,* Bible lingo for ripped all to hell.

Yancey took a jab or maybe they just spooked on their own but in two shakes the air was full of fish — all jumping for the light bulb. The first dozen landed in the boat, then one hit the glass and it shattered. Yet even in the dark they kept coming, and didn't stop till Yancey was ankle deep in fins. He damn near fell overboard but caught himself on the gunnel at the last second.

He wiped fish slime from his eyes, then hollered, "What the hell we gonna do with all these mullet?"

Mullet got guts like burnt gear lube. If you can stomach the cleaning, they're pretty good dredged in egg and stone-ground cornmeal then deep fried in bacon grease. But let 'em lay too long, or freeze 'em and thaw 'em out, you might as well call the cat.

"Cuss 'em and kick 'em and they will all be flounder," Rut said.

"You speaking in tongues or you lost your mind?"

"Don't you know your Scripture?"

"My grandpappy was a preacher," Yancey said. "He never said nothing about mullet, flounder neither."

"You must'a never talked to Meatball Jenkins," Yancey said as he cut the twine with his barlow and unraveled one of the gunnysacks. "Throw a half dozen in the washtub. We'll sack up the rest, ice 'em down and take 'em to Moses in the morning. We owe him something for the boat. By the way, Merry Christmas."

"How you know it's Christmas? You ain't got a watch."

"Oh, it's Christmas. Listen."

Up at the Friendship Baptist, they could hear a new song, wafting along the sea breeze, freshening now with the tide change, ebb giving way to flood as it had twice each day since God hung the first full moon.

Go tell it on the mountain, over the hills and everywhere

Go tell it on the mountain, Jesus Christ is born.

"I reckon you're right. Merry Christmas to you too, old buddy," Yancey said.

They shook hands, would have embraced but they were too deep in mullet to move.

"Can I buy you a drink? I got a pint in the truck," Rut said.

"Where you get it? We too young to drink."

"Prince Washington on Sam's Point Road. He's laid up drunk on his porch most every day. He'll go buy anything you want for a two-dollar tip."

Yancey put his ear to the wind and sang with the faithful best he could.

Once I was a sinner, I sinned both night and day

I asked the Lord to help me and He showed me the way…

The water rippled, the wind sighed, the porpoise circled and came back alongside. In the starlight they could see him, grinning that fool porpoise grin and rolling his eyes. He rose up on his flippers, slapped his jaw on the water — *pop, pop,* "Hey y'all, let's keep fishin'."

Rut threw him a mullet. They had plenty to spare. The porpoise caught it midair. "You done got we mo' mullet than we can stand. Go long wiff you now, git."

The porpoise knew Gullah, heard it every day his whole life. One quick swirl and he was gone.

Rut swung the skiff around and the boys rode the new tide back to the dock.

Chapter Two

Suddenly Afraid

And the tides ran and the winds roared and the ocean sighed and moaned like it always does, that low and lonesome vibration you can feel and almost hear if you love it like Rut did. There were wars and rumors of wars. There was famine, pestilence and earthquakes in diverse places. And the sea still moaned.

Fast forward a dozen years.

Rut knew there was trouble when he saw the buck fawn in the crotch of that live oak tree. Most of a buck fawn, anyway, pitiful rags of skin gnawed to sinew, tendon and bone. He knew there was trouble and the little hairs at the nape of his neck were looking 'round for trouble before he even knew it.

He was not normally afraid, not after the bears and the buffalo and the boars. And that crackhead in the beer joint he slapped upside the head with a bottle of Chablis way too good for him. The crackhead went down, Rut straddled him and beat his head upon the concrete till the bartender and the cook pulled him off. The crackhead came to holding a knife. But Rut came up with a pistol, end of the conversation.

The crackhead floored his flap-fendered Ford around Rut's house at 2 a.m., cutting doughnuts and firing a 12-gauge shotgun into the air, but he dared not breach the door. Of course, they arrested Rut for that, two cops walking right in unannounced when the air was blue with reefer smoke. Assault and battery and "affray," which meant waving a pistol about in public.

They took his pistol for evidence but as they could not find the magazine and it would not fire without it, they had to turn him loose. So far as assault and battery, they figured the crackhead had it coming. After that, Rut feared neither man or beast, nor any company of men.

But this was something different, way down on that Beaufort County rice dike when he was following up a wounded boar pig with his 30-30 Winchester.

He'd seen a bobcat on this very trail only the week before. Wild country, the bob had likely never seen a man so close. They met almost face to face — equally surprised. Cat eye met his eye for fifteen seconds, but fifteen seconds is a very long time looking into the eyes of a wildcat, like looking back a half-million years. Then, with a quick side step, the cat was gone into the spartina cane and black needle rush, gone like a puff of gray and yellow smoke. Thirty pounds of muscle, fang and fur, that bob could have easily hauled the fawn to the crotch of that oak.

But he saw the pugmark, bigger than a biscuit, almost as big as a Waffle House waffle, a clean print in the mud of the trail. Then he knew what his gut told him when he first saw the fawn in the tree. It was not a bobcat.

He forgot all about that wounded pig. It would not go to waste. The man who was no longer afraid was suddenly very afraid again, fear rising in his throat and laying heavy on his tongue like a tarnished penny. He knew big cats prefer to attack from behind so he double-checked his rifle, while his heart hammered in his chest, while his pulse washed in his ears like hurricane surf and sweat ran down his back like ice water. Putting one foot behind the other, he inched backward down the trail toward his boat, praying he did not trip and fall.

Halfway there, he noticed the birds. Forty minutes after daybreak, when the woods should have been alive with the calls of red birds, thrushes and wrens and the rice field canes riotous with migrating red-wing blackbirds.

But all was quiet, as quiet as death.

It was the dark of the moon, the flood tide at daybreak and now his boat was swinging in the freshening ebb, tethered to a pine snag in a canal dug by enslaved Africans and indentured Irishmen so long ago. He was very happy to see it, even happier when he fired the motor, happier yet when he slipped the line, turned and idled along with the outgoing tide.

He was a man of great faith, Washed in the Blood, as they say down here. He came to Jesus late but he came to Him hard, plunged into the river by the elders of the First Union African Baptist while hungover and reeking of a woman, in an ebbing tide like this one, so the river would carry his sins out to sea where they would only bother the porpoises, who are happy fools anyway, as they have sex for fun.

Yes, Rut was Washed in the Blood but alas, the Good Book says, "The tongue is an instrument of hell," and his vocabulary briefly overcame his religion and though there was only God there to hear him, he yelled:

"What in the Freaking Sweet Jumping Jesus did I just see?"

Washed in the Blood

Way off in the distance a fish crow called, first bird he'd heard all morning.

"Uh-uh, uh-uh," it said.

The Old Man held him captive with the poetry of his words, with the pauses between his words, with subtle intonations. Nighttimes he looked deep into the flickering yellows, blues and greens of driftwood fires; daytimes he stared off into the middle distance like he was reading his script off the sky.

"Back on Roseland Plantation when I was a boy, the panthers would squall like women way down in the swamp. You ever hear a woman squall, son?"

He'd heard his mammy pop off a time or two, and one time she got so mad, she fainted dead away. But she never squalled. "No, sir," he said.

"My grandfather kept the hands up all night feeding bonfires at the edge of the stockyard. Whenever a panther squalled, the meanest coonhounds would shiver and roll their eyes and back up to the fire till their tails smoked and stank," the Old Man said.

Thus the panther skulked the boy's nightmares, prowled his dreams, quickening his step when he was in the big woods heading home at sundown. He would forever see those terrified hounds, forever smell the stink of their fur.

But there are no panthers here, just ask any government game biologist.

U.S. FISH AND WILDLIFE SERVICE 5-YEAR REVIEW

November 2010

Species reviewed: *Puma concolor couguar*, Eastern cougar

South Carolina – Schoepf (1911) lists the puma among the early mammals occurring in the State. Audubon and Bachman (1851) believed the puma present in South Carolina as late as 1851. Warden (1819) believed it extirpated east of the Appalachian Mountains by that time. True (1883) listed the puma as "probably extinct," but Golley (1966) reported a kill in the Camden area in 1916 (Appendix B). Nowak (1976) cites several recent unverified reports.

The puma is classified as a State-endangered species and individuals are protected from take under the State ESA. The DNR has no confirmed evidence of pumas and believes that a wild, native population does not occur in the State. The State does not keep a puma sighting database. The State of South Carolina does not provide license, permit, registry, or standards for the care of captive pumas, therefore prohibiting ownership of pumas in captivity within the State. Despite this, the DNR believes there may be 25 to 50 pumas in captivity, but a Clemson University forestry professor is aware of 100.

Thatcher et al. (2003, 2005) developed a GIS habitat model for potential Florida panther reintroduction sites in the Southeast, but did not identify sites in South Carolina. Jordan (1993, 1994) identified an area in coastal South Carolina that could support pumas, but did not meet the Thatcher et al. (2003) minimum area criteria. The DNR identified two areas of potential puma habitat in the northwest part of the State (Sumter National Forest and adjacent areas and lower Savannah River). Deer densities of >30 deer/mi^2 occur throughout most of the State, and the statewide population is about 800,000.

Such is what Rut read online, while Washed in the Blood.

"Pappy, I think there is a panther way up New River."

"Well of course there is Sonny! Did you have to almost graduate from Carolina to know that? You remember those stories about 'em when I was a boy?"

"Yes, Pappy, I do."

His pappy was dead ten years and that was all he could wring out of the air while there at the grave, and at his grandfather's grave, and his great-grandfather's grave too. The last of the camellias gave scant scent. And the wild azaleas had yet to bloom. So the air was short on fragrance and stories, way back on a ridge by another rice field.

Used to be a church there but it burned a hundred years before and only gravestones remain of the pirates and the parsons alongside the grim and rusted iron crosses for the Confederate dead. The dead speak better when the magnolias bloom on a hot night with no breeze when the scent makes you dizzy and you swear you could cut the air with a dull skinning knife. You keep your eyes peeled for the copperheads while doing graveyard walking and gators bellow way down in the swamp like giant, toothy bullfrogs, and the spirits softly whisper in your ear.

He visited two or three times each year; hoped to be planted out there too, but wasn't in any great hurry. When they buried his grandmother, they hired a crew to clear the gravesite with bush-hooks, as no machinery was allowed near the stones. They were eaten up by chiggers and ticks, but got her in the ground anyway. It was a wet year and the casket floated in the bottom of the grave, bubbled as it sank. When his mammy saw that she said, "If y'all bury me way out here, I'll come back and *haint* you!'

His mammy was painful enough in life. Nobody wanted to chance her ghost. So they bought her a plot in town.

Chapter Three

When the Sea Wind Told Lies in Her Hair

Mudbank Mammy's, where they swept up the eyeballs come closing time. A concrete floor, creek-side beer joint, where you walked through the splayed and sagging door into an instant 1967, where the jukebox was free, the gumbo made you sweat, and the girls occasionally got deep into the Jose Cuervo and danced naked upon the bar.

Posters on the wall: Grateful Dead at Fillmore East; 20th Annual Round Up and Wild Pony Swim at Chincoteague, Virginia, proceeds from pony sales to fund the local volunteer firemen. Another advising, "Please roll your own marijuana, our pharmacist cannot roll it for you."

A few chipped and wobbly Formica-top tables, no two the same, an indifferent collection of barstools. Body heat was most of the heat and beer-sign neon made most of the light.

Mudbank Mammy in the kitchen, sweaty and rotund with a voice like a Savannah ship-channel foghorn. An old blister was slinging rum drinks and a goodly crowd was there.

Washed in the Blood

The waitress was mighty fine, washed ashore here for reasons Rut did not know or understand. Jen was a willowy blonde beauty, butched-off hair, with a little ski-jump nose and eyes as bright as the blue neon behind the bar. She could have stepped right out of Robert Redford's Sundance catalog, except for the extravagant tattoo of a Phoenix bird rising from ashes on her left shoulder, diagonally across her back, way down to where he wished he could see.

She had a dweeb of a boyfriend, the son of a professional mime, she said, and a ninety-pound crossbreed bulldog, which a gator snatched up when it stopped for water at a pond behind the beach. They heard a yelp, then a great splash and it was gone. Rut wished it had been the son of the mime, not the dog.

Rut was Washed in the Blood so Jesus forgave him for wishing that. No getting loose from being Washed in the Blood sometimes.

King David, God's favorite in all the Old Testament and the direct ancestor of Jesus Himself, was the inventor of Rock & Roll. He took a rock and rolled Goliath. David was also a musician, authored the Book of Psalms, "Yea tho I walk through the valley of the shadow of death" and all that.

Ladies loved him, as you might suspect, especially Bathsheba, who artfully deployed herself naked beside a rooftop bathtub a few doors down from the palace. Trouble was, she was Uriah the Hittite's wife. As they did not have cable news in those days, no problem.

But "The Eye that Never Sleeps" was watching.

King David sent Uriah the Hittite off upon some hopeless mission and upon the conclusion of hostilities, poor Uriah was pierced through and through, leaking bad.

King David mitigated the widow's grief as best he could. He

flat knocked the bottom out of that gal and she bore him a son who died a few days after birth.

God's payback.

Another boy, Solomon, was reportedly the wisest man in the Bible, but was actually as dumb as a pine stump, as he had nine hundred wives and concubines. He was a poet, most noted for the immortal line, "Thy navel is a goblet that needeth not wine." Had Solomon drunk wine from all nine hundred navels, he would have perished from acute alcohol poisoning.

The Good Book does not mention any tattoo. Rut thought of whiskey in her navel and how he'd lick it up: Tennessee, Irish, Scotch? Bailey's, yes, that's it! Bailey's Irish Cream.

She stood next to him at the bar and leaned into him till he felt her firm, cupcake breasts hard against his arm. "What's wrong, Rut? You got something on your mind?"

"You," he said.

He was William Rutledge Elliott IV, but most folks called him Rut. He'd grown up on this river sunburnt, barefoot, cut-foot, free and wild. His pappy was a waterman, his grandpappy was too, and his great granddaddy was a Confederate Navy officer. Rut ran a barge, soggy Navy surplus, bumping sea island to sea island carrying roofing tin, propane bottles, lumber as needed. Mostly he hunted and fished, tended a flock of laying hens and a big garden, legal and otherwise.

"Honey, you wouldn't believe it."

"Try me," she flashed a million-dollar Sundance smile, perfect Chiclet teeth. "I go on break in five minutes. Want to smoke a joint?"

He did.

They met in the dappled moonlight behind the dive while the sea wind told lies in her hair. She pulled the joint from her tubetop, from that little hollow between her breasts and cupped a Bic lighter against the breeze. She took a hit, held it ten seconds, then slowly let the smoke roll from her lovely little nose.

She passed it his way and made sure her finger tips lingered on his, if only for an instant. It was warm for late February and the joint smelled of frangipani and woman and faintly of kitchen fry grease.

The intoxication came with a rush. He did not know if it was the marijuana, the woman, or both. Didn't matter.

"You gonna tell me?" she asked.

He passed her the smoke. "Panther," he said.

"You saw a panther?"

"No, just the track. And a dead deer in a live oak."

She tried to laugh but as her lungs were full of reefer smoke at the time, it broke loose like a sneeze, a cough and a fart put together, one of those high-pitched lean-ass girl farts, like an errant note on an alto sax. Smoke blew from her mouth and nose and maybe her bung. It took a bit before she could speak. Hippies love clean air, but dirty air will do if there's dope smoke in it. "Dead in a tree? How'd it get up in a tree?

"Panther," he said.

The back door blew open and Mudbank Mammy boiled out into the yard florid and sweating, waving a long-handled serving spoon. "What the hell is wrong with you?" She jabbed her spoon this way and that for punctuation, exclamation marks mostly. Strap two '64 VW hubcaps on her considerable chest and she could have auditioned for a Wagnerian opera.

"You're stinking up the whole damn place! I got customers in there! Move downwind!"

Lettering on her stretched, stained and spattered T-shirt said: "What if the Hokey Pokey is REALLY what it's all about?"

Capum Pete was Mudbank Mammy's husband, for a while anyway, till he showed up drunk one night too many as she was writing the evening specials on the whiteboard. She hit him atop the head with a No. 10 Griswold cast-iron skillet, then, as he struggled to his feet, jabbed him in the eye with her Magic Marker. Capum Pete kept clear thereafter, taking his ease in the evenings upon his own porch, watching the river flow with his one good eye.

Capum Pete had learned and forgot more about New River than most men ever knew. In his younger days, he ran a long string of crab-pots there. He'd break out a six-pack, steam the crabs in an oil drum over a wood fire, pick out the meat for the restaurant, a process that would eat up another full day and at least another six-pack per bushel picked, a tedious undertaking. A man might gut, skin and quarter a full-grown buck deer in less time than it took to pick a bushel of crabs.

Mudbank Mammy mixed in crushed Ritz crackers, fine chopped onions and green pepper and seven secret spices then stuffed the culinary mojo back into the vacated crab shells. Labor intensive but value added, as three live blue crabs worth forty cents each, a sliced tomato alongside and a Red Stripe beer to boot would fetch up twelve bucks. Baked like a pizza, four hundred degrees for fifteen minutes and served on folded sheets of the *Savannah Morning News*, Mudbank Mammy's devil crabs would make a vegan smack his lips, jump up and down and holler. They were as renowned as her gumbo.

Rut suspected she did not like him much, which mattered more than you might think. But he liked her well enough. He liked her other ninety-seven personalities just fine too.

He had most of an English degree from Carolina and it served him well on rare occasions. Shakespeare said Julius Caesar was heckled by a soothsayer on his way to his assassination: "Beware the Ides of March!" Ides were the slack-water days, the middle of each month.

Julius did not listen.

Rut didn't either.

It was March 15 when he came calling upon Capum Pete.

It was a long lonesome track off a long lonesome road, a tunnel of green — oak and pine and black cherry, Spanish moss dripping like the Tears of Jesus.

Rut was left-handed and his writing predictably suffered. After failing two cursive tests, his third-grade teacher demanded mitigation. He was to choose a Bible verse and write it one hundred times. He chose John 11:35, "Jesus Wept."

At the time, he thought he was getting off easy, but he'd been seeing Jesus weeping ever since.

He brought along a six-pack of Bud, the island coin of the realm, lest it be a bag of pot, of which Capum Pete did not partake, claimed not to anyway. But he kept a bag around most times. "Son," he told him once, "if you got reefer, you always got friends."

Rut rapped on the trailer house door, no answer. It was a single-wide from the mid-50s, soft around the windows and doors, saggy at the soffits, held together mostly by a tin-and-plywood wraparound porch. It would not likely survive the next hurricane. An out-of-balance ceiling fan wobbled, thumped and whooshed inside. A radio squawked country music, AM country music, the worst kind: "Does My Daughter Call Him Daddy?" "You Don't Have to Call Me Darlin, Darlin." "My Get Up and Go Done Got Up and Gone."

Rut rapped on the door again.

The six-pack was sweating and he had no way to keep it cold. He walked around the porch to the water side. "Capum! Capum!" he hollered.

There came a grunt like a wild boar hog grunts when he catches your scent.

"*Ah-wonk!*"

Rut rounded the southwest corner of the trailer house, where the scrub palmetto fronds grew up to the porch railings, to the river side, where the maritime brush was whacked back just enough to discourage the copperhead snakes. Capum Pete's skiff was hauled upon the riverbank, half full of green-scum rainwater. The case was off the motor and floating in the bilge. Herons and egrets had roosted upon the wreck and left it artfully decorated with splat — like a Jasper Johns abstract.

"Capum Pete, where you?"

And empty beer can hit the porch floor, *ta-ching*. "Naming Chinese babies!" Capum Pete hollered.

He was stretched out in a rope hammock. It wasn't really rope, rather the belly of a shrimp net stretched between two barrel staves, three or four empties on the floor beneath him. He rose on one elbow and affixed Rut with a bleary-eyed squint. "Hey, Sonny, what you up to?"

"Brought you some beer," Rut said.

"Mighty white of you," Capum Pete said. "What you want?"

Rut worried a can from the plastic, put it in Capum Pete's hand. Pete was a man-and-a-half tall, half-a-man wide. Knobby elbows and knees, thinning gray hair, a patchy grizzled beard, skin hanging like wrinkled burlap from a lifetime in the sun, shrimping, a stint in the Coast Guard, then crabbing until he retired to the shrimp net hammock. He was drawing Social Security, likely the minimum, but he paid no rent and it was enough to keep him in beer. He sat up, put his feet on the floor.

"Nothin', really," Rut said.

"Don't bullshit me boy." He popped the top, took a long pull, smacked his lips. "You never bring brew lest you want something."

"Maybe you never see me except when I want something," Rut said. "But I always bring you brew."

Pete lapsed into nautical lingo. "Aye Laddie, tis true. The grog is always dear to me heart. But belay the jabber. Why Laddie, do ye hail me now?"

He took another pull on his beer.

Rut eyed a beach chair folded against the wall, plastic webbing frayed and bleached by the sun. It might hold his weight. "Mind if I sit down?"

"You might as damn well, so long as you're interrupting my afternoon nap. What time is it, anyway?"

Rut did not wear a watch or carry a phone. Sun and moon and tide told him what he needed. "I got no earthly idea," Rut said, "but the sun is over the yardarm. Can I have one of these beers I brought you?"

"Help yourself," Pete said.

Rut grabbed the chair, which sagged and crackled but held. The beer tasted good. "You know more about that New River country than anybody."

The first of the salt-marsh mosquitoes came a whining as the sun began its long western slide, slipping off toward the rooftops of Savannah, a dozen miles across the broad marsh flats, canes gold as grain for the harvest while an old man and a too-soon-to-be old man drank and jawed.

"Upper river is pretty stable," Pete allowed. "Not much change since that big oxbow broke through the narrows. The lower is stable too, but the middle is a bitch, sandbars shifting all the time. I ain't been up there in a coon's age."

"I was up there last week and it's gone completely to hell," Rut said.

"How's that?"

"You remember how in 36 miles of river, you could see only one house?"

"The big house on Red Bluff Plantation."

"Yep, but now you can see two."

Pete snorted. "Shittin' progress," he said. "Fixing to kill us all yet."

Rut grabbed a second brew. "You mind if I ask you somethin'?"

"You might as well."

"You won't think I'm crazy?"

A coon came out of the marsh, poked around looking for

fiddler crabs. It was too early for fiddlers so it found none. Way out in the Intracoastal channel, a Yankee yacht was blowing smoke and throwing a mighty wake. They came through twice each year. In March, they were all northbound now.

"Son, you are already batshit crazy. Everybody knows that. Don't matter what I think," Pete said then stretched out again upon the hammock, wiggled his toes, Sperry Top-Siders, split out and worn all to hell. He wore no socks.

Rut hesitated. The question rose in his throat. A third beer might have helped, like the joint did with Jen. "You ever see a panther up there?"

Long pause. "Did you see one?"

"No, but I saw a track."

"Bobcat," Pete said.

Rut shook his head, held out his left hand. "Big as this."

"You get a picture?"

"No," Rut said, "I was just happy to get my ass out of there with no scratches."

Pete chuckled. "I never saw no panther." He paused. "But I saw a bear."

"You saw a bear?" Rut passed him another brew, the next to the last.

"As I live and breathe. Swam right in front of my boat." Pete squinted, through the years, trying hard to remember the details. "About a hundred pounds, maybe a hundred and a quarter, 'bout as big as a sack of potatoes. A young male, I figure. This time of year, likely looking for romance."

"If there's a bear up there, there could be anything!"

"You got that right, Sonny. Keep your eyes peeled for a zebra." Capum Pete wiggled his toes again. "Speaking of romance, tell me 'bout that lil' hottie down at the beer joint?"

"Nothing to tell," Rut said.

"Space cadet. You see her propeller beanie?"

"One on each tittie," Rut said.

Thus, their confab lasted five beers and ended as it had begun, with another boar-hog snort. "Don't you lie to me, boy!"

Rut left with the last brew, almost too warm to drink, but not quite. He popped the top as he slid in behind the wheel. It was gone before he got home.

Chapter Four

Once Upon a Crooked River

It was wild and wonderful country, and a river so crooked it passed the same spot three times. Heading up from the sea, you pass the big blue tanks on Elba Island in the Savannah channel to your starboard quarter. A great looping bend and those tanks are dead ahead. Another switchback and the tanks are to port. There was a lighthouse there in the olden days, and the keeper's lonely sister was seduced by a Portygee sailor who swore he'd come back in a marrying mood. He didn't and she met every incoming ship, flag by day and lantern by night for the next 40 years. There's a statue of her down on River Street. Locals shake their heads in sad sympathy. "She waited on that ol' boy till she petrified."

The wandering channel left a broad floodplain, so vast there seemed no end to it, and in some places the view across the spartina, needle rush and cattail marshes was like looking out to sea, no land in sight. Slaves and later indentured Irishmen labored with barrows and shovels to turn these marshes into productive farmland with canals, dikes and dams for cultivation of rice.

Carolina Gold, they called it, not from the color of the grain, but for the money it made. But the Yankee Army burned the rice mills and barges, freed the slaves. About the time everybody got Free Labor figured out, the Great Sea Island Storm of 1893 breached the dikes and let in the sea, poisoning the fields for the next generation. By the time the fields were fit to farm again, cultivating and harvesting were mechanized and local mud would not support the new steam tractors, which more resembled locomotives than agricultural equipment. Production moved to firmer ground: East Texas, Arkansas, Louisiana. There were still patches here and there in South Carolina and Georgia — worked with tracked machinery, put up in small batches for boutique restaurants and the tourist trade, mostly along the Savannah River and up the coast to the North Carolina line. One farmer even trademarked the "Carolina Gold" and grew yellow rice.

Rut knew all about slavery, as much as any white man could know. Elvira Mike, the granddaughter of a rice field slave, raised him from the cradle. She taught him the old spirituals in his grandmother's kitchen during winter when the old wood range rumbled and roared. And he learned the ring shout, too, the dance of praise going clean back to Africa. Black Baptists could dance in church, so long as they didn't lift their heels.

Now Rut was heading up the river again, spinning his skiff around the oxbow bends, keeping to the outside of each curve where the water was always deepest, with Yancey alongside him. They had not seen each other in years, still Yancey was the one man he trusted to cover his ass should he go back, and he knew he was going back from the very first when that big cat spooked him off the rice dike.

Each brought a pump shotgun, and the tide and time and the guns were stuffed full. Repeating shotguns can hold up to five rounds but, according to the law, each is restricted to only three shots for hunting waterfowl. To limit the number, a wooden dowel the length of two shells is inserted into the magazine. Both men had removed their dowels, no problem, as they weren't hunting ducks or geese, not even marsh hens. So each shotgun was loaded to the gills — five shots apiece.

Yancey liked double-ought buckshot, nine big pellets each time he pulled the trigger. Rut preferred single-ought, twelve smaller blue whistlers exiting the muzzle above the speed of sound. Either would rip some serious ass, man or beast. They had developed their tastes back when they were boys hammering hogs and deer, and had not deviated from their respective leanings.

Rut found the little side creek on the north side of the river that led to the rice canal, cut the throttle and eased along with the flood tide.

"Watch out for Sherman's Revenge," Yancey said, referring to old timbers washed down from the old Seaboard trestle.

Another bend in the creek and they saw some wreckage, a burnt-off piling with timbers attached — casually floating mayhem that would cut the bottom out of any boat run by any damn fool. "Old burnt railroad trestle," he said.

"No man, it's part of that pontoon bridge Sherman built over the Savannah River when Fighting Joe Wheeler was hot on his heels. The Yankee bastard burnt it once he got his army across."

Rut knew about Fighting Joe, who after the war swore allegiance to the Yankees, joined the U.S. Army and later fought alongside Teddy Roosevelt at San Juan Hill. When he saw the Spaniards quitting their positions, he got so excited he forgot which war he was in. He stood up, waved his hat and hollered, "Come on boys, we got dem Yankees on the run!"

Rut shook his head. "How in the hell did that thing get way up here?"

"Hurricane of 1893. Hell of a surge, eighteen feet maybe."

The creek straightened out into a canal, dug straighter than straight slap though the middle of an island. "I reckon it don't matter where it came from," Rut said, "so long as I don't run over it in the dark."

"Easy enough to remember where it is," Yancey allowed.

Rut spat over the side. "Sum-bitch floats up and down the creek, different spot each time I see it."

Nothing to jaw about there, Yancey changed tack. "Ain't this the island with the busted-up still?"

"Yep, axe holes in all the barrels."

A gator saw them coming and slid off a mudbank. He was maybe ten feet and stretched most of the way across the canal. He submerged as they passed over him and remerged in their wake. It was early for the gators to be out but there he was.

"A full-grown by-God," Yancey said.

They tethered the skiff to the same snag Rut used earlier, but as the tide was still in the flood, Rut rigged an anchor off the stern quarter, threw it far as he could, took up all the slack and cleated it short. There was a stout deadfall across the canal. They could go no further. The men stepped ashore. The bank was steep and stepping from the skiff to dry land was like stepping across a curb from street to sidewalk, but the nearest curb was forty miles away.

"You cover my ass," Rut whispered. He carried his shotgun

in one hand, a day pack in the other. Inside the pack was a cheap aluminum pot, a big spoon, a jug of water and a sack of plaster of Paris. He was fixing to make a cast of that pugmark. He knew a pugmark did not make a panther, but a panther damn sure made a pugmark.

The trail crossed the island, then ran alongside the canal. They passed the oak where he had seen what was left of the fawn, nothing there. A dozen more steps when Rut froze, eased his pack to the ground, cupped his free hand to his ear. "What in the hell is that?" he whispered.

Diesel engines, not a steady laboring throb like a generator, like a pump — which they sometimes used this time of year to drain a rice field before planting for duck hunting in the fall. In between the revs and rattle came the occasional crack of falling timber.

"Golf course," Yancey whispered back. "I read it in the paper. Building another freaking golf course. Reckon that's what spooked that cat of yours out of the big woods?"

Golf course. There were eighty-five in the county already, nearly sixteen hundred holes total as some had twenty-seven instead of the usual eighteen. Nothing like it for real estate sales. Sell lots along fairways, around lagoons dug to build greens and tee-boxes while fertilizer and weed killer runoff poisons the salt marsh, kills oysters and thins the fish.

They struck up the trail where Rut saw the pugmark but there was no pugmark. "It was right there! Damn rain!"

"It didn't rain that damn much. To hear you tell it, it was big as a Waffle House waffle and six inches deep."

Rut wanted to cuss. There is nothing so satisfying as a good cuss when you most need it. But he was Washed in the Blood, so he choked it back.

Yancey shifted into Gullah, "You sho' dat ain' yo 'maginate?"

"I know what I saw," Rut said.

"You still got any?"

"Any what?"

"That shit you was smokin' that day. I want some of it."

"You can kiss my ass!" Rut turned on his heel and headed back toward the boat, slipping and sloshing along the muddy trail. No reason to be quiet now.

They passed that oak again and that's when they heard it — a wheezy thud like a deerhound makes when it jumps from a pickup, four paws on the ground and great blast of breath, *a-honk*.

Yancey grabbed Rut's forearm so hard his fingernails broke skin. Yancey wasn't Washed in the Blood. So, he said: "Jesus Freaking Christ! Did you see that?"

"See what?"

"He come right out of that God-damn tree! Black," he said, "That sum-bitch was *black*!"

"Black?"

"Black as Toby's freaking biscuits," Yancey said.

Chapter Five

Chickenshit Tea

Rut fed the chickens and did a quick count, thirty-three or thirty-four, close as he could get, them scurrying the way they do. Maybe one short, that big old barred-rock hen about at the end of her laying? Onions, rice and celery, she'd be mighty fine upon the woodstove, cooked long and slow, but now just a few feathers on the wind. The coons, hawks and owls minded their manners whenever Rut was home, as he warmed their asses up with fine shot and they knew the drill. He never intended to kill them, but sometimes he did. Which he always regretted.

All God's critters got to eat.

He put an inch of straw in the bottom of a bucket, picked the eggs, lay them carefully upon it, an even dozen, clean, brown and perfect. He took a sand spade and scraped a hatful of manure from the henhouse floor. He threw it into the bottom of another pail, drew water and sloshed it around a bit: chickenshit tea for his reefer plants.

The man could grow some serious reefer, but good seed was hard to get. "Yea," the Good Book says, "God created them, He created them male and female." He leaned heavy on that verse when gazing upon Jen, that tattooed wonderment. Sometimes when he thought of her, his britches grew and his head hurt like he'd been eating ice cream too fast.

But to other seed. While most plants have both male and female parts, *Cannabis* plants, both *indica* and *sativa*, are either male *or* female. The bump and the buzz come from THC, essentially a female plant sex hormone. Once the female blossoms, it expects to be bred, like Jen, even if she did not yet know it. If a guerilla gardener identifies his male plants early, pulls them up, and insists his neighbors do the same, the female gets increasingly frustrated, produces more and more THC till — *bammo* — two good hits would stick your dick in the ground.

And this is good, yes, it is very good. But unfertilized females produce no seed and a man needs seed to make a crop. So Rut kept two gardens, one harem of females in amongst his sweet corn, the other along a fence line way down in the woods where he let the males mature to do their work. Yes, the deer gave the seed crop ever-living hell. But if he tried to fence it, the Coasties would spot it from the air. While not rescuing mariners in distress, the Coast Guard flew these islands daily, taking note of illegal trash dumps, illegal docks, illegal anything, including dope. He pissed on the bases of the plants instead. Piss is high in nitrogen and deer don't like human piss. They hated panther piss even worse, but Rut didn't have any. Not yet, anyway.

About the end of February, he'd shuck the seeds from the seed crop buds, lay them in a tray. Incline the tray, tickle the pile of seeds and little leaves with cardboard torn from a rolling paper cover and the perfect round seeds would roll down to the bottom lip of the tray with a satisfying little rattle. The leftover leaf was entirely smokable, good enough for casual company anyway. But still, not all seeds were viable. You don't want to fool with something that won't grow.

Put a thimble full of seeds in a shot glass, add water and set the glass on a windowsill where it catches long afternoon, early spring sun. Dead seeds float, so skim them off and throw them in the woodstove. The others will swell and split, emitting a single tiny bubble before sinking to the bottom of the glass.

Big love from thereon.

A sheet of paper towel, folded in half. Lay the germinated seeds gently side by side, a quarter inch apart, then roll up the towel, stick one end in the shot glass water, set it back in the window sun. The towel will wick up the water and create the perfect humidity for those little darlings. One day, two days, maybe three, unroll the towel to find the seed husk further split, a slender root on one end, a pair of blessed green leaves on the other. With a sharp eye and a steady hand like the best brain surgeon, Rut lovingly placed each into a Dixie Cup full of "potting" soil, appropriately named. After the harvest, this was his favorite part of the ordeal.

And it was an ordeal. Early March, those forty Dixie Cups were sequestered in a cold frame on the south side of the house, in full sun. The cold frame was a rectangular box of boards, three-feet-by-five, dug halfway into sandy island soil. It was covered with salvaged window-sashes, no two the same, but when he kept the sand wet and the sun beat down, it was mid-July beneath the glass.

And the ordeal continued. At six inches, Rut transferred the seedlings to Folger coffee cans, or Maxwell House, one of the few things that did not matter in this precarious enterprise. Finally, at two feet tall, Rut tortured the bottom out of each can with a hand-crank can opener, upside down before they were finally placed in a carefully and well-fertilized hole amongst the sweet corn or along the fence line way back in the woods. The cans were left around each stalk, which kept back the cutworms.

But it was March and the plants were still in the coldframe when Rut was feeding chickens, picking eggs, thinking about women and panthers and sloshing up chickenshit tea.

Rut carefully lifted each window sash and dribbled a couple of ounces on each plant, not too much or the nitrogen would burn them sure as any herbicide. More art than science here. The right amount promotes an explosion of leaf. Four months, some of his plants would be higher than his head. He'd cut them back once, twice, to keep them hidden in the corn.

The chickens were cooing and clucking, scratching up the cracked corn he threw them when he turned toward the house. Two dozen eggs in the fridge already, he left the new ones on the porch. Jimmie Jenkins or somebody would snag them, leave him some crumpled bills in the bucket. Wasn't much money in a yard flock but selling extra eggs helped with the feed.

The house wasn't much, a four-room Gullah shanty from about 1910 when the island's oyster business was booming. But slop from the paper mill and sugar mill crept up the waterways from Savannah and now slop from the golf courses poisoned the oysters and threw thousands out of work. Just like rice production, there were still productive beds were a man might pick all he could eat, but there was only one commercial shucking shed in the entire state.

Rut bought the house and an acre on the marsh for back taxes some years ago. Windows and roofing tin rattled in the wind but the chimney was sound, though made of salvaged brick. A woodstove cooked his meals and kept him warm in the winter; there was a two-burner gas hotplate and always the river wind. An air conditioner leaned precariously from a bedroom window, employed only on the sultriest summer nights.

He rooted around in a cooler on the kitchen floor, came up with a couple of scoops of ice for his whiskey. He didn't have an ice machine, ice trays either. He filled up his cooler every other day at Mudbank Mammy's. Some days Jen was there.

Rut didn't carry a phone but he had internet to a hundred dollar laptop he bought in a pawnshop the same day he bought a well-used revolver. The revolver was rusted up inside. He stripped it down and cleaned it with steel wool and an old splayed-out toothbrush on his kitchen table, upon a mat of back issues of the *Savannah Morning News*. The laptop was loaded up with porn-site cookies, creamy-skinned Eurasian girls tag-teaming Congolese refugees mostly, which he deleted right after surfing them all. It was too old to be password protected and he squirmed at the thought of anybody going through it should he be lost overboard, or fall prey to any other danger attendant to his life choices.

He'd fronted Yancey a half-pound of his best weed, nearly a thousand bucks. Yancey was good for the money, Rut knew that. But Rut was hot on a panther's trail and when the time came, he wanted Yancey to owe him a big favor. He took a long pull off this whiskey, rolled a smoke while he waited for his computer to boot up, longer as it found his internet provider, www.hargray.com, the Lowcountry Communication Specialists, whose signal came to him along a mile of corroded copper wire half the size of a raw angel-hair pasta noodle, underground most places, but sometimes crossing a road hung from the limbs of live oak trees.

He went straight to his inbox. There was an email from his dear friend Anya, an engineering student in the Ukraine posing bare-breasted and holding a book and a pair of reading glasses. Perky titties maybe like Jen, titties with strawberry nipples. But the book was in Cyrillic, instant dyslexia to his eyes. She was looking for a lifetime husband and asked him to send her U.S. dollars for an airline ticket from Kiev, certified funds. It might have even been true, as they were shooting each other in Kiev that year, as in most. And that poor girl was so desperate, she mass-addressed to thirty-seven accounts, that he could see anyway. And all of them started in an E.

Delete.

Another offering a deal on daily delivery of the *Savannah Morning News*, a patent impossibility, even though back issues often came in handy.

Delete.

Gold and silver bullion at a few bucks over spot price?

Delete.

And then the one he was looking for.

Mr. Elliott, thank you for your recent email. Though the Department continues to receive reports of large cats in South Carolina, we believe most of these were misidentified bobcats, otters and dogs. There is no credible evidence of the existence of the Eastern Cougar. Your report of a "black panther" is especially problematic. While both the African leopard and the Mexican jaguar occasionally exhibit melanistic individuals, there has never been a recorded instance of a melanistic Puma concolor. Thank you for your interest in this matter.

Sincerely,

Jerry Drinkwater
Assistant Biologist for Endangered Species
South Carolina Department of Natural Resources

Rut leaned back in his chair, took another hit off his joint, chased it with a generous slug before he exhaled. Both smoke and whiskey burned good.

"Chickenshit tea," he said.

Nobody heard him but God.

Maybe God told Jesus.

But maybe not.

Chapter Six

A Siren's Song

He had a load bound for Bull Island, passengers and freight. Lumber, roofing tin, tools and a couple of Mexicans to run them. Maybe they were Mexicans, maybe Guatemalans or Hondurans, hell, these days Rut could not tell them apart.

Rut spoke passable Spanish, present tense mostly. He could get directions, buy a Corona or a Dos Equis, make change and rent a room should the situation avail itself. But these men spoke a rapid-fire approximation of the mother tongue, about every fifth word, *chinga*, Spanish for horizonal relations, a term employed in the extreme vernacular by carpenters from the Yukon to the Great Ganges. Seems you could just not make two boards join up right without it. Jesus was a carpenter before he took up preaching for a trade.

Surely Jesus didn't cuss.

Maybe that's why He changed professions.

Bull Island was a couple thousand acres, formerly the private getaway of stockbroker Alfred Lee Loomis, who rode out the Great Depression in high style. Loomis diverted millions to a private passion, not whiskey and dope, as many rich men had done before and will do again so long as there are men with more money than good sense. Loomis built his own private electronics lab in a place called Tuxedo Park and in an age before transistors, printed circuits and such, invented a gadget that measured the speed of artillery shells. Then he took a partner and produced the first practical military radar. Einstein and Fermi came calling and picked his brain and adapted some of his notions to build the ultimate gadget, the A-bombs they dropped on the Japs. But by and by his wife caught him poking his secretary and raised so much hell, he retreated from public life and turned Bull Island over to his son, who stocked it with bison, Sicilian donkeys and Axis deer. The deer hit the ground running and were never seen again, though the whitetail on the other islands thereabouts grew some strange and wonderful antlers for the next dozen years. One bison bull went rogue, swam over to Palmetto Bluff and attacked his reflection, predictable enough, but his reflection was in the windshield of the game manager's Ford. The car was totaled but the loss was not covered as an attack by a rogue bison was deemed "an act of God." The bison's head still hangs above a fireplace in a bar there, Buffalo's Bistro.

Loomis Junior's kids had no interest in the place and sold it to another rich Yankee who stocked it with quail. Dick Cheney hunted there once and the cops shut down the waterways for miles around for safety reasons. Now Rut was hauling that load of lumber and roofing tin. It looked like they were building a new kennel for the pointers.

Rut ran a thirty-six-foot surplus Navy landing craft, officially an LCVP — a landing craft, vehicle, and personnel, commonly called a Higgins boat, from the Louisiana yard that built the first of them to service moonshine stills in the Bayou country during

Prohibition. Flat bottom, big-ass diesel and a ramp on front, Higgins boats put the first men ashore at D-Day so one could damn sure land lumber and tin on Bull Island, no bridge, no problem. Five hundred bucks for half a day's work, easy money. Rut nosed against the bank, kept the engine at idle and in gear. The carpenters unloaded supplies and tools while the wash from the big prop swirled and sucked up great clouds of river bottom mud. That chore accomplished, he wished them *adios* and backed away into the channel, swung the wheel toward home. That first beer was gonna taste about perfect. He had a reefer in his shirt pocket but could not get it lit there in the wind. No cabin on a Higgins boat, he had a big beach umbrella rigged above the steering station to keep him out of the worst of the sun.

Bull Creek twisted around the back of the island, treacherous and narrow some places but it steadily straightened, widened and deepened till it joined the Cooper River where it was twenty feet deep and a quarter-mile across. He was back in the Intracoastal channel, easing on home when he saw that Yankee yacht, southbound, unusual for that time of year.

About sixty-five feet, ketch-rigged, with a Zodiac dingy in tow, a couple of bicycles on the foredeck, yellow diesel cans, red gas cans and blue water cans tied to the railings, a rainbow to port and starboard.

A ketch is a double-mast boat, the aft mast shorter than the foremast. A schooner, the aft mast is taller than the foremast. Rut sailed single-mast boats — sloops.

Lots of idle Yankees, *Trustafarians*, Rut called them, burnt out third sons, assorted grandsons and great-grandsons of the captains of industry, spent the summer in Mystic Seaport or Sag Harbor, bumped on the down the Intracoastal to winter in the Bahamas or the Keys, a regular parade some days. They were never very fast

Washed in the Blood

but held fuel and water for five hundred miles, longer with jugs as deck cargo. They lit up the ship-to-shore VHF radios with their vile intonations five months each year. Rut would rather hear fingernails on a chalkboard than a Yankee on VHF. There was this girl from Long Island who once grabbed his ass outside Mudbank Mammy's in broad daylight in front of God and everybody. She was blonde and bleary and barefooted with nice titties, but when she chanced to speak, Rut lost both interest and ability. When Capum Pete got wind of it he famously proclaimed, "Sonny, you *could* have stuck *something* in that gal's mouth!"

But Rut did not. He had his standards.

A couple of porpoises were riding the yacht's bow wave, likely too close to the hull for the skipper to see them. Right common in these parts. But then a woman came out of the cabin, walked forward, bronze from the sun, she was bare-breasted with a bright blue skirt to her ankles and a great frizz of rust-red hair. She stretched forth her arms, palms up, like Rut imagined Moses did when he parted the sea. Or more likely Moses' momma when she set him afloat on the crocodile Nile. Dear God, save this child!

Sometimes Rut felt like Moses, cast adrift on dangerous waters. No crocodiles here, but gators aplenty, even in saltwater. And sharks? Sharks made Rut all itchy inside because sand sharks might get confused in the surf, mistake a hand or foot for a splashing mullet. They meant no harm, but it would still cost a man forty stitches, sometimes some nasty post-op infections, as sharks seldom brushed their teeth. Hammerheads and tiger sharks in deep water didn't care. Old Shorty Wilson fell off his sailboat in Calibogue Sound. He was wearing a life jacket, so he did not drown. They found the body washed up in the marsh, et off clean up to his waist. Sea gulls had taken his eyelids and Shorty went off into Eternity legless, assless, with a wide-eyed look of total surprise.

Rut thought all this in a flash, in the few seconds it took for a pair of porpoises to leap at that woman's command. Again and again, they leapt clear of the water, arching through the air, gracefully into the water again with hardly a splash. Her lips were moving but he could hear nothing above the yammering of his big diesel. He throttled back, shifted to neutral, killed the engine and cupped his hand behind his best ear against the wind as the Higgins boat swung down the tide.

Some kind of wailing chant, a tremolo like some Choctaw maiden mourning a lover killed in battle? A Hawaiian priestess calming a volcano? Rut had never heard anything like it. He should have remembered his world literature class at Carolina, the chapter in *The Odyssey* wherein the beautiful naked women sang to sailors from the jagged rocks, luring them to certain death upon the breakers. He should have remembered how Odysseus plugged his men's ears with wax so they could not hear, how Odysseus alone could hear their cry, how his men lashed him to the mast and ignored his thrashing and cursing, his gnashing of teeth, his orders for them to beach the ship so he might rush into the sirens' arms, and when the wind quit as if at the sirens' command, his men put their backs to their oars and rowed the ship to safety. Rut should have remembered all this, but he did not.

He docked his Higgins, fenders out, double-tied and auto bilge pump on as usual, grabbed the beer cooler from his truck, jumped in his skiff, fired the engine and took off after the ketch. He popped his first brew soon as the big skiff got onto plane but he saved the joint in his shirt pocket. They didn't call it "the old thigh-opener" for nothing.

He caught up with the ketch at anchor in the mouth of New River. It was a mile wide where it met the Intracoastal, a perfect anchorage, plenty of water even at low tide, protected from all but a full gale out of the west and far enough from the main channel

Washed in the Blood

where a man need not worry about getting run down by the fuel barge making regular trips — day and night — to the Marine Corps air station north of Beaufort. Any given day, there might be three or four yachts, power and sail, riding the hook at the mouth of the New.

Didn't matter how much money a Yankee yachtie had or how long his family had it, they were universally and notoriously cheap. They would never pay dockage at a marina if they could anchor up for free. They might stop at Skull Creek, Harbour Town or Thunderbolt for water and fuel, or to take on liquor and groceries. They used bicycles for their errands and seldom called a cab, even in a rattling rain.

Rut throttled down and circled the ketch, *Plan Sea* out of Newport, Rhode Island. Nobody on deck. He knew better than to come alongside and step aboard. Two hundred years after the British Royal Navy supposedly put an end to international piracy, there were still pirates in the Caribbean. Despite tales of Captain Kidd's and Henry Morgan's riches, most pirates were a sorry lot. Calico Jack stole rope and cloth. Anne Bonney and Mary Read were more interested in snuffing each other than plunder. Even the notorious Blackbeard's last offense was stealing a load of French sugar. Modern pirates were no exception — low-down opportunists. They would board you at night. They would not shoot you if they could help it, as that would leave a bloody mess. They would throw you overboard instead, steal whatever you had, then sell your boat to cocaine runners, who would use it only once, then burn and sink it at the end of the run. Only a fool left U.S. waters without being armed, well-armed most instances. Most gun companies offered firearms in "Marine Configuration," rot-proof plastic stocks and rust-proof stainless steel or nickel-plated actions. Even here, Rut had seen the Coasties stop a sloop in the Savannah channel, a 50-caliber Browning manned and at the ready, bullets the size of kosher dill pickles. They were kosher all right, hot lead at three thousand feet per second, cut a boat clean in half quick.

Rut circled the ketch, killed his engine and hollered, "Permission to come aboard, Captain?"

A voice barked from below deck, "Permission denied!"

Chapter Seven

Jah be Praise

Rut ran his skiff up the Intracoastal Waterway toward Beaufort the next afternoon trying to get that bare-chested woman off his mind. He checked the New River anchorage en route and the Yankee ketch was gone.

Thirty-seven miles by land from All Joy Landing, but only twenty-eight by water, some of it big water, very big water indeed. The Intracoastal twisted and turned behind Hilton Head Island, narrow, shallow and indifferently marked, then broke out into Broad River, aptly named, some three or four miles across and more than twenty-five miles long, all the way up to fresh water in Jasper County. Looking northwest from the mouth of the Broad, you could not see land and looking the other way, the nearest beach was the coast of Morocco, thirty-six hundred odd miles away. You could not see that either.

French Huguenot Jean Ribault visited the area in 1562. "There is no finer or fitter place," he noted in his ship's log. "Here all the navies of the world might be anchored." A deep estuary, a nine-foot tide, salt marshes richer and more fruitful than the finest Iowa corn ground, a scattering of emerald-green timbered islands and miles of broad sandy beaches.

Beautiful but deadly, Port Royal Sound has killed more men than many small wars. Drowned outright most of them, but there was hypothermia, sharks like poor old Shorty Wilson's, waterspouts and the occasional lightning strike. Scuba divers dove for fossils. There were lots of fossils that fetched up a fair price but some divers never came up again.

And more men than many large wars too if you factored in the French and Spanish and English and Indians in their historic hundred-year hatchet fight.

Somewhere off the north end of Hilton Head Island, way out in the watery vastness, there is a red buoy, not easy to find without radar, and Rut had none. But he had to find it anyway. From that red can, turn ninety degrees by the compass — due east — a dozen miles to another red — a steel tower this time — off the sizable mud bar at the tip of Parris Island. Round that tower and head up Beaufort River, along a channel fairly well marked with a jumble of buoys, as it was both the Intracoastal and a ship channel for the Port of Port Royal.

Look at a chart and you can see that mud bar, bigger than the whole of Parris Island, where they train Marine recruits. About 1962 an Air National Guard P-51 crashed out there. Salt ate up the airframe quick enough but not that massive Allison V-12 engine. A dozen years later, Rut was working a long string of crab pots in Port Royal Sound when he spied two boaters in distress, wildly signaling from the scant safety of an oyster shell rake. He cocked his outboard, blubbered into shallow water and took them aboard. They had been cobia fishing up the Broad River, planning to sell their catch to the Blue Channel fish house when they decided to take a shortcut across that mud bar. Needle in a haystack? They hit that engine block a glancing blow, which split the hull stem to stern. Only five feet deep, they did not drown but they lost the boat, the motor and all their fish. Rut was selling crabs to Blue Channel, so he carried them there when he was done pulling his pots and left them wet and muddy upon the dock.

The Port of Port Royal was a confusion and continuing conundrum. Though sea captains from Ribault to Blackbeard to the present day proclaimed it the finest harbor on the East Coast, the only time it was ever seriously used was during the Federal invasion of 1861, when the Yankees patched up ships and men shot up during the siege of Charleston, which was longer than the siege of Stalingrad and nearly as bloody. So many sailors, soldiers, storekeepers, barkeeps, runaway slaves and whores on Hilton Head, it took over a century for the population to surpass what it had been in 1865. And then the demographics were much the same, excepting the runaway slaves. These days there were the last of the Gullah rivermen, the vegetable farmers, fruit-stand vendors and fishmongers, with the occasional crackhead distributed amongst them.

But to the port. In South Carolina, the State Ports Authority has a hammerlock on planning, building, maintaining and operating all three of them, a multibillion-dollar enterprise. The Authority is run by a board, almost all of them from Charleston, and — by God — there would never be another port that would ever be allowed to compete with their hometown. So when Beaufort politicians started agitating for a port in "the finest natural harbor on the East Coast" the State Ports board offered to build them a bridge instead — a bridge across the Broad River that would cut forty miles off the trip to Savannah at absolutely no cost. A free bridge some four miles long? Why, hell yes! So, State Ports built that bridge and they built it too low for a ship to ever get through and they named it for the state senator who took the deal.

Washed in the Blood

    A generation later, when that first bunch of politicians had gone on to their just reward, the next bunch took up the cry for the port once again. They were good and honorable men, mostly. Rut sold reefer to many of their grandsons, granddaughters too. But by that time, the only possible location was at the confluence of Beaufort River and Battery Creek at the village of Port Royal. So they built a port there, cleverly running the dock and warehouse about twenty-five degrees to the bank rather than parallel to it. Thus the port could never be expanded. Try to add onto it westward, you'd be high on dry land, to the east, you'd plug up your own ship channel. The port was never used to capacity, leased out instead to various private interests, the export of kaolin clay, of government-surplus powdered milk and most notably for the import of furniture-grade logs from the Amazon Basin. The logs came in as deck cargo on tramp freighters, and as there was no machinery for unloading them, the ships were careened and the logs rolled overboard, then dragged upon the bank by D-8 Caterpillar tractors, along with attendant four-foot iguanas and tarantulas bigger than your hand, mighty lively times in the village for weeks after each unloading. Though no pythons were reported, the iguanas licked up both the wharf rats and the local feral cats.

    It was a lot to think about but Rut had time, spinning down the Broad River, crossing Port Royal Sound, rounding the tip of Parris Island, then up Beaufort River for a powwow with Yancey, who owed him money for a half-pound of reefer he had spotted him. Yancey was living on a boat in Factory Creek, so named for the oyster cannery that operated there in the olden days. They had a boiler to steam the oysters, and when Rut was a kid, he lived by the whistle. When it blew in the morning to call the shuckers to work, it woke him up for breakfast. When it blew at noon, it was time for lunch; at one, it was time to get back to class; and the knock-off whistle meant suppertime. He never wore a watch. Didn't have to.

Rut actually didn't want Yancey's money. He was fixing to chase a panther and he did not want to do it alone. The water was flat and the tide was right and aside from a light chop off the Parris Island bar, the running was easy.

Port Royal village and the defunct port was on the way. Aside from the monolithic concrete monument to politics, pride and folly, it was an interesting town on a dead-end road, as the best ones generally are. There were clusters of Victorian age cottages, most of them with a least one boat in the yard. There were shrimp docks, a funky little marina, an ancient spreading oak where the Emancipation Proclamation was read to a crowd of slaves in 1863, a couple of clapboard Baptist churches and the school was old enough to be on the National Register. The centerpiece of the community park was a sea buoy that had drifted ashore clean from Scotland, and a sheet-metal, red-headed mermaid welcomed visitors at the town-limit sign, but Rut tried not to think about that, as it reminded him of the bare-chested woman who sang to porpoises. But more importantly, there was the District Office of the Department of Natural Resources, Marine Division. Rut printed out the chickenshit email he got regarding no panthers, and carried a copy in his pocket.

Rut tied the skiff, slipped the dockhand five bucks, walked up to the dockmaster's office. It was a quarter mile to the DNR and Rut figured to slip the boss a ten-spot for use of the golf cart they kept for running errands around the village. It took an act of the legislature but now carts were legal on city streets but not on state highways, which made sense. However, a honking big-ass ATV, four-wheel-drive with turn signals, wipers, horn and seat-belts weren't legal on either, which made no sense at all. But Rut didn't have time to think about any of that right then. He just needed wheels and it was pushing 3:30 p.m., government quitting time in these parts, unless it was a warden laying up all night trying

Washed in the Blood

to catch a night hunter jack-lighting a deer or working his reefer patch. The dockmaster sported modest dreadlocks and a Bob Marley T-shirt that had seen better days.

"How you do, Sir Rut, sir?"

"No Woman, No Cry," Rut replied. "How you, Desmond?"

Jamaica is a little island way out in the deep dark blue on the other side of Cuba. There are too many Jamaicans on Jamaica and many have taken to the sea. They run barges and boats and marinas from Miami north till it gets too cold for them to stand it anymore, halfway up North Carolina, generally. As the old Gullah rivermen slowly passed away, Jamaicans gradually took their place. They stuck together, jabbered their patois, jerked their goat meat, beat steel drums, turned Bob Marley up loud and smoked copious amounts of "de breath ob Gawd, mon," rerolled into the cigar wrappings. It was a constitutional right, they reckoned, as the First Amendment clearly states, "Congress shall make no law regarding the establishment of religion, nor prohibiting the free exercise thereof."

Some were citizens, some had green cards, some had nothing but busted out shoes and raggedy britches. But within six months, all of them had debit cards, cell phones, and dimpled and smiling white girlfriends with tattoos.

Jah be praise mon!

There may have been some no-count, low-down, suck-egg Jamaicans, but Rut never met one, and he never could sell them reefer. They always had plenty. And there was his neighbor's cleaning girl.

You ever have Jamaican gal?

And as he was wrestling pulse and breath, she said, *Jamaican gal, she kill you, mon.*

Rut did not want to die just then, so he politely declined though often later wished he had chanced it.

He remembered the drunk old blisters staring into the oyster-roast fires when he was just a boy, how they chuckled wistfully: "Boy, you try black, you never go back." And how another said, "The blacker the berry, the sweeter the juice."

Which scared ever-living hell out of him, destined for being Washed in the Blood like he was.

Rut held out a twenty-spot, Abraham Lincoln, that bastard bisexual who burnt his people out. The bile rose from Rut's gut to his throat whenever it came to mind, but not often, *Jah be praise!*

"Desmond, can I bum your cart for a few minutes? I got to run up to the DNR office."

"Meester Rut, suh, yo money ees no good here! Keep yo money mon!" He paused, shook his head. "Meester Rut, you watch yo-self round dem blood clot, mon."

Blood clot? Oh yes, the police.

Rut promised he would but he did not know he was about to run into a right fit specimen of female law enforcement.

The district office was a tin pole building with a brick façade and an office on the front. There was a bicycle with fishing rods parked in the shade and as the zeal for apprehension often exceeded navigable water, there were any number of mangled watercraft parked out back. There was an elderly black man at the counter, a trim female warden behind it. Her hair was blonde and braided and reached the middle of her back. She wore a spray can of mace, a pair of cuffs in a little Velcro holster, a Glock automatic and her nametag said Callahan.

The black man nodded at Rut's appearance and spoke to the

woman. "They tell me I gots to have a fushing license now. I wants to buy one."

"Saltwater or fresh?" she asked.

"Saltwater, ma'am."

"OK, that will be eleven dollars and fifty cents."

The old man fetched an old-time, snap-open change purse from his pocket, the kind ladies carried in their bags years ago. He peeled out ten soiled and wrinkled dollar bills, plunked down a dollar and a half in small change, pushed it across the counter.

"Very well, sir, do you have a copy of last year's license?"

"No, ma'am. Dis is my firstest. I never knowed I needed one."

"Well, how about a driver's license?"

"Ma'am, I wants to fish, not drive."

Officer Callahan was clearly getting frustrated. "Do you have any other form of identification, sir? A letter addressed to you? A power bill? A phone bill? A bank statement?"

"What you need all dat for, ma'am? I just wants to fush."

"Sir, I just have to know you are who you say you are!"

The man threw up his hands, strode to the door. "Who else would I be? Who else wanna be me?"

Officer Callahan shook her head, turned to Rut.

Rut learned long before how to read a woman's eyes. Hers were green with little flecks of pecan mixed in. Being a cop didn't matter. She liked him.

"And what may I help you with, Mr ...?"

"Rut," he said. "You can call me Rut."

Her eyes lit up again. "Rut" is breeding season amongst the deer, mid-October to mid-November, mostly, depending on the weather. But Rut was in rut most of the time.

"And what can I do for you, Mr. Rut?"

Rut slapped the copy of the email on the counter. It was short and to the point and she read it in about thirty seconds. "This is the agency's position," she said. "I'm in enforcement, we don't get into policy. And you saw a *black* panther?"

"No, I just heard it jump from the tree."

"So you *heard* a black panther jump from a tree? How does a black panther sound when it jumps from a tree?"

"Like a big-ass coon dog when he jumps from the back of a pickup."

She smiled again. "Does a *black* coon dog sound differently than a spotted one?" She was in full cop mode, almost.

"I don't know, ma'am. I never seen a black coon dog."

"So, you are a local."

"Yas'sum, since about 1700. Where you from?"

"Oconee County."

"Way up in the mountains?"

"Yes, sir!" she said with a hint of pride.

"You got panthers up there too, right?"

She pushed the paper back across the counter. "Here is the agency's statement. What more do you want?"

There were a couple of security cameras recording the proceedings. Rut pointed with his nose like an Indian. "Them things got sound?" Rut had no Indian blood so far as he knew but he pretended whenever it suited.

"No," she said.

"What gonna happen if I shoot a panther and dump it on your porch?"

"You don't even know where I live," she said.

"I could drop it off here," he said. "You could pick it up."

"I would not do that if I were you."

"You mean you would put the cuffs on me for killing an animal that does not exist? How 'bout a dinosaur?"

"I know of no statute protecting dinosaurs. Like I told you, I am in enforcement."

"I got one more question," Rut said, "and I will be on my way."

She seemed disappointed at the contemplated end of the conversation, so Rut took a chance: "You want to slip outside and smoke a joint?"

The Earth stopped spinning; the Earth stopped revolving around the sun. Not really but it seemed so for ten seconds.

"Sir, you are speaking to an agent of the law."

"I am painfully aware of that already," Rut replied. "I'll consider myself under arrest ..."

So they passed the joint and he did her on the tailgate of a broke-down government truck. She bent her sweet ass over, dropped her government britches but left her government boots on. Her government pistol and cuffs and mace lay in the government dirt.

And she screamed ... she bit an eight-ply spare tire and

screamed like a panther.

Back at the marina Desmond gave him the fish-eye. "You do OK wid dem blood clot, mon?"

High on reefer and endorphins, Rut's feet were barely touching the ground. His mustache still smelled of Officer Callahan and, damnit, he called her "baby" and she called him "baby" and he never got her first name. Not yet, anyway.

"Desmond, no problem, mon.

Desmond shook his head with a great and profound sadness. "Oh, Meester Rut, I know you! You watch yo-self round dem blood clot, mon."

Chapter Eight
Sleeping on the Slant

Back in the skiff, the outboard humming and back up on a plane, brain humming too. Get a big skiff up on a plane, then throttle back, the way to run in flat water, mighty easy on the fuel and sensibilities. Up Beaufort River, his knees still a little weak from that tailgate rendezvous, the best times in life being unexpected and generally undeserved, he was one happy man, even with that panther skulking around in the back of his brain the way it was.

He reckoned Jesus did not approve but He never had blue-eyed, braided female cops, or tailgates either. He remembered that Gospel story when the whore Mary Magdalene washed Jesus' feet, and Rut often wondered what Jesus was thinking when she dried them with her hair. It was nothing he could ask a preacher about but he thought about it very privately and often.

The riverbank from Port Royal to Beaufort was a jumbled boneyard of history. The old tabby fort built by the Brits in the 1730s, the phosphate mine from the early 1900s, the bridge named for the sheriff who turned to voodoo to make himself

Washed in the Blood

bulletproof-, the grand old town itself founded in 1711, ransacked by the Indians in 1715, bombarded by the British during the Revolution, looted by the Yankees in 1861, shook by earthquakes, blasted by hurricanes, burned in a great fire, it somehow survived and was now noted by sundry Yankee magazines as the most beautiful small town in the South.

And it was.

The grand old mansions of the cotton barons remained, mostly now bed and breakfasts and boutique hotels for the tourist trade, and the whole of downtown was devoted to discretionary spending, not a God's thing a man actually needed. Looking for a cast net? Drive out Martin Luther King to the Walmart and buy one made in China.

It broke Rut's heart, but good bourbon and homegrown reefer helped dull the pain. Lots of saltwater therapy did too.

Finally, there was Woods Bridge over to Lady's Island, named for the state trooper gunned down by bank robbers in the late 1960s. Lady's Island was named by the Spanish in 1526, after the Holy Virgin, back when there were virgins hereabouts. Some men lusted after virgins, a great curiosity, as every other enterprise required experience, many with resumes. Rut never understood it.

Factory Creek is on the other side of Woods Bridge and there Yancey lived aboard an oceangoing trimaran, three hulls covered by a deck big as a tennis court. With a black dog named Captain Flint, no taxes, no rent, no lawn to mow, Yancey came and went by a dingy and kept his truck at a boat landing near the island side of the bridge. Various women could not come back without a call. Yancey had a cell phone for that purpose and that purpose alone. Now that he had a half pound of Rut's reefer, the phone popped off right regular. Some women said they would not trust Yancey with a worn-out shoe. Others asked "right or left?"

But, *What the hell*, the boat was gone!

Sailed away? Sunk?

The engine had not run for years. It was a Volvo Penta three-cylinder diesel with left-hand rotation that required a backwards prop. The Swedes were perfectionists and notably eccentric, an entirely cantankerous race. They built three-cylinder cars, too, two stroke engines about the size of an old Evinrude thirty-five. If you blew a Volvo marine diesel, you were obliged to rebuild or repower with another Volvo, or you would be buying another prop that turned right like most single screws did, an expensive proposition.

Wait a minute, there it was, hauled onto the bank next to Geechee Von Harten's shrimp dock, and from the looks of it, there was one hell of a party going on. When Yancey saw Rut easing up the creek, he hailed him with a wave and a holler. Rut could not make out the words above the outboard. The air over the boat was hovering blue with marijuana smoke, his marijuana, he suspected. More than suspected, he knew damn good and well it was his, or used to be, anyway.

Rut tied his skiff at the shrimp dock and walked the bank to the shindig. There was a motley collection of derelict lamp cords plugged end to end running from the side door of the shrimphouse across the dirt parking lot to Yancey's boat. A set up like that might run a single sixty-watt light bulb or a ten-inch Walmart fan but hardly both. A rickety stepladder led to the deck, about six feet up now that the trimaran was grounded, about six deep in women, from what Rut could see standing in the mud.

"Permission to come aboard, Captain!"

It was the second time he asked that day.

"Well grease yo' ass and slide on up," Yancy hollered back. "Step aside, lads and lassies," he hollered to his guests, "sunglasses only! Do not attempt to gaze upon him with the naked eye! Behold the Prince of Panthers!"

There was no need for illumination in broad daylight and a freshening breeze was better than any Walmart fan. The scant wattage ran an automotive battery charger that was wired into an automotive CD player that squawked out the Grateful Dead through automotive speakers pulled from junk car doors and laid upon a derelict sailboat dock, two of them from high-end GMC products, Bose systems, the best speakers in the world, "Uncle John's Band" at the moment.

God-damn, well I declare, have you seen the light?

Their walls are built of cannon balls,

Their motto is "Don't Tread on Me"

It was particularly appropriate for a man bucking up to established authority, the reefer garden and the panther and all. Coming off the last joint and Officer Callahan the way he was, Rut could not help but notice.

Damn smart-ass Yancey! Rut raised his hand as he bested the ladder and stepped upon the deck. Captain Flint, the black dog, remembered him, whined, wagged and nosed his hand. As the bleary-eyed assemblage considered his arrival, he said, "No need, no need. Eye protection is only optional. Reports of my radiance have been greatly exaggerated!"

A well-worn blonde in a red string bikini way too small for her age was prone upon the forward hatch-cover, soaking up the sun. She rose on one elbow and grinned, "The Prince of Cougars?" she asked.

If that don't beat all? He thought. *Ain't that the way it always goes: Either no women whatsoever, or too damn many?* But she had this cute little bubble butt and a pair of dimples at the small of her back. Two women in the same day? Once he had three but that was years ago.

Rut bucked up. "No ma'am," he said, "I may be the Prince of Panthers, but I'm the King of Cougars."

She slipped on a pair of Bahama Mama sunglasses, made in China and marked up tenfold, pursed her lips, shot him a smile, clenched the muscles of her ass. "Yancey was right," she said. "These help."

"You're mighty easy on the eyes, yourself, ma'am. But tell me, do you wear those things to bed?"

"Try me," she said.

Soon as he could, he cornered Yancey. "Hey man, you got somewhere I could wash up?"

"There's a bucket and soap below deck. Towel too if you ain't too fussy. Why?"

"Sardine sandwich for lunch. Hard on the social life, you know."

"Never known you to eat sardines."

"Every chance I get," Rut grinned.

Yancey shook his head. "You dog, you. Follow me."

Illumination below was a single kerosene lamp, flickering, smoking, stinking and sputtering from a bracket screwed into a bulkhead, all available wattage being consumed by the sound system on deck. Hauled on the bank the way it was, everything aboard was about fifteen degrees off level.

Yancey explained. "Bottom was grown up bad so I hired Jimmy Logan and his semi-wrecker, Big Ben's Brother, to haul it onto the bank. It was going good till she fell off the rollers and punched this big-ass hole in her bottom." Yancey peeled back the floorboards and there was a rat's nest of splintered plywood and fiberglass, big as a bushel, a hole punched clean through the starboard side of the middle hull. Rut saw the river mud through the breech, fiddler crabs scurrying around below.

Rut poured a quart of water into a shallow pan. "So now what?"

"Got to bum a generator and a saber saw. You find that soap?"

"Yep. Where's that towel?"

It was wadded atop a bunk. Yancey shook it and a big old roach skittered away beneath a dubious sleeping bag. Roaches had been recently rehabilitated, like killer whales, which were now orcas, dolphin fish were now mahi, and the real estate wizards told their Yankee clients these weren't roaches at all but palmetto bugs.

Yancey considered the hole again. "Two sheets of five-eighths marine plywood, a box of three-inch brass screws and a case of twenty-two hundred marine caulk and I could fix it in a couple of hours."

Rut dried his face, threw the towel back on the bunk. "Is it eighteen hundred or twenty-two hundred?"

"Damned if I remember, but you know, that sticky shit."

Captain Flint rattled down the stairway, lay his head on Rut's knee, looked up with his sad dog eyes. Dog eyes were an evolutionary development, if you believe in evolution, although Rut wasn't sure, Washed in the Blood as he was. The eyes said, *I love you, feed me take care of me and I'll take care of you.*

"So, meanwhile you're sleeping on the slant?" Rut asked.

"Yep, ain't too bad so long as you keep your head uphill."

Shuffling and rhythmic thumping from the top deck. Somebody dancing. Woman in the red bikini, maybe? A stirring in Rut's britches, look out, boy!

But business before pleasure. "You got money for that dope?" Rut already knew the answer.

Long pause. "Not yet."

Rut nodded toward the upper deck. "Your good-timing friends smoke it all up?"

"Not yet, but they're trying hard."

Rut was fixing to spring the trap. "Maybe I got a better idea."

"Oh Lord," Yancey said. "Lay it on me."

More thumping and shuffling on deck. "Keep the money if you ever get it. Help me with the panther instead."

Another long pause. "How in the hell do I help you with a goddamn panther?"

"Not sure yet."

Yancey shook his head. "You scared, ain't you?"

Rut was scared, alright, but hated to admit it.

"How long you been going up New River?" Yancey asked when Rut didn't answer.

"Not sure. Five or ten years, at least."

"And how many times you seen a panther?"

"I never saw one, jackass. You did."

Yancey stood up, worked his way around Captain Flint, his head still on Rut's knee. "I got a better idea, for now at least."

Yancey dug through a box of miscellaneous truck parts

Washed in the Blood

generally found on a live-aboard boat, an ancient foghorn, a couple packs of D-cell batteries, a mossy bottle of sunscreen, Band-Aids, fishing twine, a couple of tattered charts. He came up with a game trail camera, dusty but new in the box. "I bought this when I was hunting Old Island. Never been used. Ought to be worth three hundred bucks."

Rut slit the cellophane with his barlow jackknife. Canvas strap to hang it on a tree, a photo card for the images. It took two nine-volt batteries but there were no batteries. A puzzlement, Chinese shit, for sure. "How do I get the pictures off this thing?"

The trap was sprung but no part of Yancey's anatomy was in it.

"Damn if I know. You got a computer, don't you?"

"Sort of," Rut said. "Who's that gal?"

That's when Yancey sprung *his* trap. "Gloria, but we all call her Deo."

"Day-o, like in the Banana Boat song? Daylight come an me wanna go home?"

Yancey grinned, he had him now. "No man, as in *in excelsis Deo*, you know, and on earth, *piece* and good will to men?"

When you're Washed in the Blood, stuff like that ain't supposed to be funny, but it was anyway. "How 'bout a beer?" Rut asked.

"Sure, bub, come on up. I'll introduce you."

"I don't think that will be necessary," Rut said.

"OK, you're on your own ... Oh ...," he said like it was an afterthought, "... She's been passed around a bit. I wouldn't ride her bareback if I was you."

Yancey went up the ladder first, Captain Flint followed, Rut boosted the dog and came up last. "Wearing a rubber is like washing your feet with your socks on," he said. "Don't you know that by now?"

"And having a good dose of the clap is like having a rattail file run up your dick. Don't you know that by now?"

"I never caught nothing, never."

"Have it your way," Yancey said.

"And thank you, kindly," Rut replied. "I will."

Chapter Nine

At Play in the Gardens of God

Up in the rice fields again, Rut was on his own. He brought his pump shotgun but left it in the skiff. On his hip was his pawnshop .38 Special, a worn but tight Smith Model-10 revolver, old enough to have a silky-smooth trigger where the bullets always go where you want. A rough trigger will ruin your aim every time. At ten paces, he could put all six shots in a circle the size of a doorknob in ten seconds. That meant a lot to him, a damn sight more than freshman physics, which he failed the first time.

Pistol on his hip and Yancey's game camera in his hand, Rut worked his way up the trail alongside the canal. First week in June, the mosquitoes were thick as blowflies on a gut-pile, which kept his free hand busy swatting them from his nose, ears and eyes. Thistles and bugs and sundry other annoyances were God's payback for Adam and Eve eating that apple, or mango or persimmon — the official account is vague. Whatever it was, it damn sure wasn't worth it, especially if it was a persimmon.

God took His ease in the Garden every afternoon, admiring His creation: birds, possums and giraffes, but especially Eve.

One evening Adam and Eve didn't show and God called them by name. Adam hollered from behind a camellia, or gardenia, or maybe an azalea, the Bible just says bush. "Over here Lord!"

"Adam, why are you hiding?"

"Because I am naked as a jaybird!"

Then the jig was up. God thundered, "Who told you you were naked?"

And there's been trouble ever since.

The pistol was loaded, the game cam was too, nine-volt batteries, those little square things that also fit smoke alarms. The photo card was a problem. One came with the camera so you could take it back home, plug it into your computer and see what you got without disturbing the set. And there had to be a set, better than the trap he laid for Yancey, damn his sorry ass all over again.

But you're supposed to buy another chip as well as the gizmo into which you plug the card, which you plug into your computer, which throws up its cyber hands in confusion, scratches its cyber ass and walks in cyber circles if not loaded up with software to read the chip once the chip is inserted into the reader and then connected to the little USB port in its side. The camera came with a CD loaded up with the appropriate programs. But Rut's computer did not have a CD drive, nor the software to run it. The ordeal ate up a month and three hundred bucks, not counting that half-pound of pot he'd likely never get paid for.

Counting and not counting. So he was not counting steps along that boggy game trail, but he was counting an easy two grand invested counting the fuel and aggravation, scared half spitless, swatting bugs in June, rather than May when the skeeters were better but the ticks were worse.

But back to the set. A corn feeder for deer or hogs, no problem, just strap the camera to a tree and point it in the general direction of the bait. But along a trail, you got to aim it right. Rut guessed a panther was a little more than two feet high at the shoulder. He picked out a straight trunk sweet gum twenty yards from the trail, wrapped the strap around it, slid it down to waist high, cinched it up. He popped in the photo chip, turned it on. It clicked when he walked in front of it.

That's when he heard a twig snap down in a thicket and his blood ran like ice water again. It could have been the panther, it could have been the bear. It could have been a deer or a wild hog or a big old tiger marsh coon.

Or it could have been nothing at all.

And then, way back in the woods, he heard a bulldozer crank up again.

His answering machine was flashing when he got back home. He let it flash while he fed his chickens and grabbed the eggs. His reefer plants were all in the ground now and about waist high, well hidden by the sweet leafy green sweet corn, which was a foot higher. They needed no attention. He let the machine flash while he rolled a joint, poured a whiskey. He sat at his desk, took a good long pull on his drink, lit the smoke and pushed the play button.

Female voice, Upcountry accent, tenuous and a bit shaky. "Ah Rut, Mr. Elliott, this is Charlotte." There was a long pause. "I thought maybe I would have heard from you by now." Then she left a number, a local number, area code eight-four-three. The next three digits looked like a cell.

Charlotte? Who in the hell was Charlotte? He played the message again, jotted down the number. He was at the bottom of his glass and halfway through the joint, a fine little fire in his belly and the reefer rolling over him like waves of warm water when it came to him. Callahan? Officer Callahan? It was Callahan, sure as shit!

How did she find him?

Oh, hell, a cop can find anything, right?

At first this gave him pause, but then encouragement.

He called her back, left a message. "Hey baby, it's Rut. The tailgate is busted clean off my truck but we got a big throw-down here on Juneteenth. I can pick you up at All Joy Landing."

They played phone tag for three days before they finally connected.

Juneteenth was June 19, an extravagant celebration hereabouts, when the Emancipation Proclamation was read to slaves around Galveston, Texas, eight hundred miles away and one-hundred-and-fifty years ago. On June 18, Union Army General Gordon Granger arrived at Galveston Island with 2,000 troops to occupy Texas on behalf of the federal government. A whole lot of Texas and damn few Yankees but the following day, standing on the balcony of Galveston's Ashton Villa, Granger read aloud the contents of General Order No. 3:

"The people of Texas are informed that, in accordance with a proclamation from the Executive of the United States, all slaves are free. This involves an absolute equality of personal rights and rights of property between former masters and slaves, and the connection heretofore existing between them becomes that between employer and hired labor. The freedmen are advised to

remain quietly at their present homes and work for wages. They are informed that they will not be allowed to collect at military posts and that they will not be supported in idleness either there or elsewhere."

Why the reading so long ago and so far away was cause for local celebration remained a puzzlement, but it was a ripping good party nevertheless, five hundred Gullah on the bank where New River met the sea: music, cracked conch, smoked ribs, fried mullet, boiled shrimp, cold beer and copious fornication in the bushes roundabout.

He picked her up at All Joy like he offered. She brought two items aboard, a starfish-and-sand-dollar-print overnight bag and a fiddle case. Pick a woman up with an overnight bag, that's a good sign, a very good sign. The fiddle case was a puzzlement.

"What you got in that case, Callahan?" He paused. "Can I call you Callahan?"

She flashed a quick smile. "Call me what you want. Just call me."

"The case?" He asked again. "You toting a tommy-gun?"

"No silly, it's a fiddle."

He slipped the skiff into gear, eased away from the dock. "We gonna fiddle around?"

She wore sandals and a white smock, a swimsuit cover-up with modest floral embroidery across the shoulders, handcrafted Mexican likely. She shucked it once she came aboard. A two-piece bathing suit underneath, not a bikini really but nice anyway, and she jiggled in all the right places when the boat hit the scant chop or the wake from another passing boat. Her yellow hair, loose from the braid now and secured by a single clasp, hung clean to her waist. You might say she had an athletic build. Not much for titties but she had a well-turned ass and the marvelous strong legs of a long-distance runner.

Washed in the Blood

She blushed at his question. "I usually don't do things like that."

"I never asked a fiddle player on a date neither ..." Rut fumbled for the joint in his pocket. "... And some white gals never been to Juneteenth."

"You know," she said. "The tailgate."

Rut offered a quick apology though he did not really mean it. "Sorry about that, ma'am."

"Please don't," she said. "Don't be sorry."

She might have been from the foothills but she was a quick learner. Rut always looked for the little things first: the boar track, the deer track, yes, the panther track, looked at the fine grains of dirt pushed up, the fine rind around the very edge of the track, the grains of the very edge of the edge. Two hours, the finest grains would be dry, two more hours, bigger ones. No, the tracks never lied but it took a damn good man to read them.

He watched her carefully. Callahan slipped into the smock as they approached the dock and handled the lines like she was born to saltwater, loose enough with the bow and stern lines so they would not part in the wake of a passing yacht, with the slack taken up by a long diagonal spring line. Rut was impressed.

Up the dock into the shack, her eyes danced during the quick look-around. She threw the overnight bag on his bed, more good sign, while he flipped on the window AC unit, grabbed a couple of cold beers, then into the pickup where they sat hip to hip on the bench seat and juttered on down the sandy track to the Juneteenth Throwdown at the county landing outside Mudbank Mammy's.

A sizable copperhead crossed the road in front of the truck, a beauty but it would kill you dead as hell. "Don't hit it!" Callahan hollered. She grabbed his knee. "Don't hit it!"

Rut eased off on the gas, swerved to miss the snake. It looked like it had some place to go and was getting there quick as it could, and disappeared into the brush on the east side of the road. "I try not to kill a copperhead if I can help it. So long as it stays away from my chickens. You know these island copperheads are a distinct sub-species?"

"*Agkistrodon contortrix,*" she said.

"No, *Agkistrodon contortrix contortrix*. Got an extra molecule in its venom."

"Bullshit," she said. She whipped-grabbed her phone, pushed buttons. "Don't phones work out here?"

"Damned if I know. Don't have one."

"Why doesn't that surprise me?"

They passed the First Union African Baptist, clapboards, tin roof and steeple, all with a distinct lean to the northwest from the hook of many hurricane winds.

"Oh, what a sweet little church! They still hold services there?"

"Yes, ma'am. I go sometimes." He did not mention being Washed in the Blood, not yet, anyway.

She shook her head. "And why doesn't that surprise me either?"

But back to that snake. Rut didn't want to miss a chance to tell a DNR man something he didn't know, even if this DNR man was a woman, and a mighty fine-looking one too. "Most vipers got neurotoxin," he said. He slipped the gears to second as they wallowed through deep sand at the corner of Church and School roads. Islanders kept it simple: Church Road led to the church, School Road led to the school and Beach Road led to the beach.

"But old Mister Copper, he got a coagulant, you know, it plugs up the blood."

"I got a degree from Clemson," she said.

"And I almost got a degree from Carolina."

"In herpetology, I assume?" She was a sassy wench and Rut loved it.

They passed the Council Tree, an ancient, moss-hung spreading oak just past the ten acres belonging to the church. Black Baptists have a strict protocol of what can and cannot happen on church property, but ten feet further, anything goes. This is where the elders stopped to council, *gossip*, on the long wagon ride home.

"Only these island copperheads have it. We used to catch 'em and sell 'em to a snake farm in St. Augustine, a hundred bucks a pop. Hundred and fifty for a big one. They milked 'em out and sold the venom to UCLA. Said it had anti-cancer potential."

"They told me you were a wild man," she said, "but they never said you stretched the truth like that."

"Who told you what?"

She laughed, tossed her hair. "Assault and battery? Affray?"

Now that was just too sassy! He swore if she mentioned his reefer patch, he'd throw her in the boat and haul her sweet ass back to All Joy, but she did not. "And now you're conducting an *undercover* investigation?"

She blushed just a little. A blonde can't hide blushing. "Rut, I'm off the clock. Nobody knows I'm here." She paused, always ready to have the last word. "But they said if I came to arrest you, just make sure you didn't have a wine bottle handy."

"OK, I'll make you a deal. You pull your pistol and I'll do exactly what you say."

She shot him the sweetest smile. "Oh, I don't think that will be necessary," she said.

He melted inside but he tried hard not to let it show.

Down at the landing, a confusion of tacked together stalls, no two quite the same. Two-by-two's, tar paper, lath and canvas, a few $19.99 Walmart Chinese pop-ups, one row on each side of the drive leading to the dock and the boat launch. Smoke rolled, music blared and the air was alive with laughter and the great Gullah tongue, as liquid as the flood tide gurgling over an oyster bank.

The dock was concrete and new, the old palmetto piling and creosote-decked structure lost in a fire several years previous when Jimmie Jenkins set a hubcap of moonshine aflame trying to keep warm one chilly March morning while waiting on a boat from Savannah to pick up his squeezings — "scrap iron," the locals called it. They had a voodoo sheriff in the old days and if you tried to lie to him, you'd slobber all over yourself.

So the corn whiskey was hidden beneath hoods, fenders and engine blocks to sell to the Jew junk dealers on Liberty Street. If the law hailed you in the river and asked what you had aboard, you could holler back, "Nothing but scrap iron, suh."

And you would not slobber.

Evonne and her daughter Jevonne were each weaving a sweetgrass basket, strong brown fingers working an ancient rhythm that came over on the slave ships, row upon row like the sea, they said,

Washed in the Blood

came over like cooking and music and cast-nets and island voodoo, still simmering in the swamp seeps and stump-holes even when most folks ain't thinking about it.

Rut chewed it all over with Miss Evonne once. They got into some serious rum one night and tried to figure out if any of his ancestors ever owned any of hers. They ran out of rum after they got it sorted out. "Evonne," he finally confessed, "if it wasn't for you Africans among us, we'd be a tribe of Norwegians."

He chose Norwegians right out of the blue as he judged them the whitest people on earth.

Evonne was right quick with her reply. "Why you would be nothing but a bunch of God-damn Yankees," she said.

The women talked as they worked and when they did not talk, they looked off into the middle distance, fingers working the whole time. They could have done it by lantern light, by candle light, by moonlight as they did in the olden times, or in total darkness, the fingers knowing what the eye could not see. They had a broad array of other sweetgrass for sale, everything from egg-picking baskets the size of your hat to the three-foot broad flat fanners for winnowing the chaff from rice.

Far gone now from utilitarian items in daily use to works of art, and priced accordingly. About time the baskets got into the Smithsonian, Rut could not afford them anymore. He bought Callahan sweetgrass earrings, little baskets the size of a dime, which was the best he could do, almost.

Jevonne fussed and fretted over Callahan, smoothed her hair, told her she was pretty and hung the earrings from her lovely lobes.

Not many white gals ever been to Juneteenth.

Rut left Callahan there with the women and ducked into Mudbank Mammy's for a couple more beers. He figured Jen was working and he didn't need to get the two of them in the same room, now or maybe ever. Men are competitive when it comes to women, but women are all sisters under the skin. If they suspect you might be even remotely interested in two of them, they'll seek each other out, gang up on you, cut your ass in private amongst themselves and you'll never ever get nookie from either one ever again. And God help you if they are blood kin, cousins are bad, sisters worse, but especially a momma and a daughter. Best not even try that trick.

Rut heard about it one sweaty afternoon when the HVAC almost worked in a double-wide in a pecan grove a little south of Waycross, Georgia. He got a firsthand report of the proceedings, and the telling thereof was not fit for polite company. He swore he was not there. If he was, he'd never admit it. It was widely reputed as the origin of the Big Bang.

But too late, Jen had already spotted Callahan, albeit from afar, hard to miss that hank of yellow hair in amongst the Gullah like it was. Jen popped two Red Stripes, slapped them on the counter, *blam, blam,* pursed her lips, did not speak. He slipped her a ten-spot and winked. She flashed more of a sneer than a smile, tossed her head, turned on her heel and stomped into the kitchen. And he'd never even kissed her — indeed a curious situation.

Back outside with Callahan, they bought ribs from Slick Rick, eight bucks a plate, rolled up a couple of rounds of oak wood to the edge of the fire, sat and ate supper. Three meaty ribs each, with baked beans, potato salad and a slice of white Wonder bread to sop up the bean juice and mop your chops when done. They joined hands with the Gullah at the setting of the sun and sang "Amazing Grace," that old hymn written by a repentant slave captain long ago.

Through many dangers, toils and snares, I have already come,
Tis grace that brought me here this far and grace will take me home.

Home. They were halfway there when they passed the Council Tree again. The woods had cooled at sundown, a dew was on the grass and the air was alive with fireflies: lightning bugs, they call them here, flitting, floating, flashing in a code you feel in your loins, but a code science has yet to understand. Rut stopped the truck, Callahan leapt from the cab, peeled her clothes and ran barefoot and naked into the midst of them. Rut followed, tackled her, covered her in the cool wet grass. They moved together and they exploded together into stardust, into everything and nothing while the fireflies hovered in holy array and flashed Yes! Yes! Oh yes!

Chapter Ten
At the Squat and Gobble

Daylight comes early in a house on the river, even when a house faces away from the rising sun, especially on a new moon high tide, which crests just as the sun clears the rim of the sea: gray blushing to peach, to orange and finally to a mirror of blue sky, and the light comes ricocheting up the bank, glistening off the Spanish moss and the undersides of the live oak leaves.

Rut reached for her but she was not there. The AC was off and the window was open and the smell of good coffee wafted in from the kitchen. Fiddle music from the porch, a jazzy version of "Deep Purple," an ode to twilight, not dawn. Rut knew it well. It was one of his mammy's favorites. "When the deep purple falls, over sleepy garden walls and the stars begin to flicker in the sky …"

The bedsprings squawked and creaked as he sat, put his feet on the floor. The fiddle music stopped. Bare feet on the floor. Callahan brought him coffee. She had on the swimsuit cover-up, that white Mexican smock, with nothing beneath. Her hair was loose, nearly to her waist.

Washed in the Blood

She put the cup in his hand, kissed his cheek. He took a single, blessed sip when she tucked the fiddle beneath her chin and began a mournful version of a most mournful song, the theme from the Civil War series, "Ashokan Farewell." As Rut watched her sway to the music, her hair swinging with to rhythm of her body, he was stricken with a profound melancholy, a great sadness when he thought of all his kin dead, his homeland laid waste, the land and the produce of the land stolen, succeeding generations impoverished. He wept despite himself, his tears coursing down his cheeks and into his coffee.

The music stopped. Callahan laid the fiddle on the foot of the bed, sat beside him and cradled him in her arms, rocking him like the big baby he was. Her hair made a cascade around his face and head, hid him briefly from the world.

"Oh honey, I'm so sorry, I just didn't know."

"Know what?" he asked through his tears.

"That you were so…." She paused, "… so sensitive."

"Don't let me fool you," he said. "I'm a mean son of a bitch."

"I don't believe you," she said.

He took Callahan back to All Joy but instead of returning to his island, he came ashore and walked her to her truck. It was a ten-year-old black Jeep Cherokee with a Team DNR sticker on the back glass. She unlocked the door, reached inside, started the engine and put the AC on max. Callahan knew better than to stick that fiddle into 150 degrees.

Midmorning and it was already so hot you could have fried an egg on the hood. Thinking about that egg made him hungry.

She wore cut-off jeans, so short the pockets hung out the bottoms of the legs and lay along the smooth tan flesh of her thighs like the floppy ears of a blue-tick hound. Her T-shirt bore a green tree frog and the words, "How many frogs must I kiss to find a prince?"

She put her arms around him. "When can I see you again?"

"How 'bout right now? We can do breakfast at the Squat and Gobble."

"Squat and Gobble? Never heard of it."

"Local joint in Old Town Bluffton. Right on 46. I'll meet you there."

"Jump in," she said, "I'll drive."

There was Old Town Bluffton and New Town Bluffton. The Old Town was a square mile laid off on a bluff overlooking May River in 1825, a refuge from heat and bugs and snakes on the rice field plantations. New Town was all stack-a-shacks and big box stores from the 1990s, when the Yankees discovered this place and the county's population doubled in ten years. Old Town and New Town together became the biggest metro area in the state, by acres, if not by population.

The AC was cranking cold by then. There was this little pine tree air freshener thing hanging from the rearview mirror. It twirled in the wind from the AC vents. It smelled mighty good, but not so good as Callahan, freshly loved the way she was. Between the morning heat and Callahan standing so close, he broke a sweat.

"I got a little errand to run afterwards," he said.

"I can drive," she said.

And she did.

Washed in the Blood

Squat and Gobble, where you sat your ass down and ate, a big tom turkey picking corn on the marquee reminded you how it's done. The owner was a rock-ribbed Republican and every serious presidential contender from George W. Bush on down kicked off his local campaign with breakfast at the Squat and Gobble. There was a mannequin behind the door, a long willowy blonde like Jen, but with no tattoos as no mannequin ever had them. But it was attired in a black string bikini and they called her Miss Thang. If you didn't know she was there and caught Miss Thang from the corner of your sight, your heart might skip a beat. Callahan's did. He watched her jump with considerable satisfaction, after she sprung his criminal record upon him so casually like she did.

The Squat and Gobble girls knew Rut, treated him like royalty, like the King of Sweden, a very important person who served no obvious useful function. And just like the Gullah at Juneteenth, they fawned and fretted over Callahan. They all must have reckoned he'd never find a woman and any serious attempt deserved their encouragement and support.

Rut liked fried eggs over easy but always ordered then scrambled when eating out so as to keep the yolk slobber off his shirt. So he ordered scrambled; Callahan two over easy. They both ordered sausage, he grits and she hash browns, and both whole wheat toast with real butter and sweet-orange marmalade.

It was good.

There was the usual clatter from the kitchen, not so bad as a Huddle or Waffle House, places you might suspect exceed the OSHA workplace noise limits, places a man should avoid hung over, plus the clink of silverware and the soft Southern murmur of small talk from other patrons. The only noise from their table was their jaws popping. Callahan broke the silence.

"What about us, Rut?"

Rut lay his fork on the corner of his plate, took a long sip of coffee. "What about it?" he asked.

"I mean, what are you thinking?"

Rut picked up his fork again. "Do you expect twenty-five words or less? Like a contest for 'Why I Like Sugar Frosted Flakes?'"

"Ten words might help."

"I don't even like freaking Sugar Frosted Flakes," he said. He was suddenly that mean son-of-a-bitch he warned her about.

But she was beautiful and he was a damn sap for a beautiful woman. Her bottom lip trembled. There was a dab of ketchup at the corner of her mouth. He reached across the table, put a hand at the nape of her neck, drew her to him. One quick lick and the ketchup was gone. Rut had had learned sometimes the best words were no words at all. Maybe that's why he never got that degree, maybe not.

The kitchen staff was watching through the pass-through window. The bacon was smoking but that didn't matter for the next thirty seconds. "Whoo-hoo," some gal hollered.

Indeed, Rut was suddenly the King of Sweden, if only briefly.

"Get a room, y'all!" the waitress advised.

State Highway 46 begins in New Town Bluffton at a shopping center called Kittie's Crossing, runs through Old Town and then along the north bank of the river where it is known as May

Washed in the Blood

River Road. Beyond the headwaters of the May, it runs alongside New River, crossing it near the hamlet of Levy, across the line in Jasper County, best known for a stop-and-rob Circle K, a seepy junkyard and the Pink Pig, a world-class barbeque joint, heavy on mustard-based sauce, a local favorite.

About halfway to Levy is Pritchardville, and at Pritchardville is the entrance to Palmetto Bluff, formerly a timber reserve and corporate hunting retreat for Union Camp, the Georgia paper giant. At twenty-seven thousand acres, it was one of the largest contiguous tracts in South Carolina with twenty-odd miles of waterfront, on both the May and New rivers. This is where Yancey said they were building a golf course. This is where the caterpillars spooked the panther out of the pine woods and into the rice fields.

There was a paved entrance lined with freshly planted live oaks. In a hundred years, it'd be an avenue of oaks like a real plantation. There was a gate and a guard shack with a guard, in uniform and carrying a big-ass pistol. There was a rutted dirt road to the right with a crudely lettered plywood sign: "Construction Entrance."

"Turn right," Rut said.

"You sure?" Callahan asked.

"Like a gelded hoss."

"How's that?"

"A stallion with his nuts cut off," Rut grinned. "All I can do is try."

"You're bad," she said. "Your nuts aren't cut off."

"And you love it."

"Yes," she said, "I do."

They didn't get far. They pulled over to let a dump truck pass. First curve, there was a three-quarter-ton pickup and another guard — Palmetto Security Services. His belly lapped over his belt and he stood in the middle of the road.

He approached Callahan's side of the Jeep, leered. "Can I help you, ma'am?"

Rut thought fast. "We heard y'all are building a golf course down here. My wife and I drove down from Atlanta. We want to look at some fairway lots. Maybe you got something on a lagoon."

That took the edge off, somewhat anyway. "You need to turn around and stop at the other gate. The guard will issue you a pass to the real estate office."

Rut feigned a great weariness. "Man, we been looking all the way from Charleston. Those real estate sharks have worn us out." He reached for his wallet. "Maybe you could let us through so we can see for ourselves before they blow smoke up our asses?"

The guard grinned, refused the bribe. But Rut knew he shared his opinion of the men in pleated khaki pants. "No, sir, they'd fire me for that."

"I don't see a pisser out here. You got a porta-john?"

Now Rut was pushing it. But he was having fun.

"No, sir, but there are restrooms at the sales office."

"No, man, for you, not me."

The guard was briefly stumped.

Rut was blowing his own smoke now. "You can always tell 'em you walked into the woods to piss and we drove in while you weren't looking."

The guard grinned, shook his head. "Hey buddy, I got house payments. They said nothing but construction equipment, so it's nothing but construction equipment. And that Jeep ain't a dump truck."

Washed in the Blood

"Hey buddy," Rut continued, "don't I know you? You're local?"

The guard puffed up, his shirt buttons about to give way. "Bradley Simmons from Hardeeville! I thought you were from Atlanta?"

"Yeah, man, but I was born in Hampton. I knew your kin."

Callahan put the Jeep in reverse, turned around. "You know his kin?"

Rut reached for a joint. "A murdering bunch of bastards," he said.

"You're not smoking dope in my car," she said.

Rut lit a cigarette instead, rolled down the window so the smoke would draft into the road wind. "They ran a fireworks stand on U.S. 17, still there.'

"Right before the Talmadge Bridge?"

"You know the spot. They robbed aging Jews on their way to Florida, dumped the bodies in the swamp at night when they were building I-95. If the gators didn't eat 'em, next morning the bulldozers buried 'em."

"You're shitting me again."

"No, ma'am, I am not. They rolled one body up in a tarp and dumped it off the Back River Bridge. But instead of sinking, it stuck up in the mud like a sore dick."

Moments later they passed a dump truck heading for Palmetto Bluff, smoking, stinking, rattling, dragging a great cloud of dust.

Suddenly Callahan was a cop again. "Anybody arrested?"

"A couple of 'em maybe. They walked into the Bucket of Blood, cut the bar into three pieces with chainsaws. Nobody wanted to say much after that."

"The Bucket of Blood?"

"That juke joint south of Hardeeville. It's a strip club now."

"You're bullshitting me still."

"No, ma'am, I ain't."

They were back in Old Town before he spoke again. "Damnit, Callahan, you got your badge?"

"Yes," she said.

"You could have flashed it and drove us right through."

"Yeah, right! Me off work and out of uniform riding around with a known scofflaw on a very cold case murder investigation?"

"Yes, ma'am."

"Why'd you want to get in there so bad?"

"Panther," he said.

She shook her head. "Rut, there is no panther."

Back at the scene of his original vexation, alongside that rice canal where he first saw the buck fawn in the crotch of that live oak tree, coming up six months now with no resolution in sight, a long time for an impatient man. But life had its compensations, de compensate, his Gullah friends said. The deacon in the First African Baptist said, *"Gawd use all-two-boff he hand."* Yup, always Jen's sweet distraction even if she was momentarily annoyed, and that rodeo with that gal in the red bikini on Yancey's boat. He almost wished he could remember her name. Gloria, that's right, *Gloria in excelsis Deo*. And Callahan, the lovely Callahan. Damn that fiddle. He'd better watch his heart this time.

There was a new deadfall across the canal, pine bark beetles scored another tree. Blocked from his usual tie up snag, he nudged the skiff into the bank and threw an anchor up into the marsh, stomped it into the mud when he stepped ashore. He would not be long, but he pushed the skiff back off the bank so it would not hang up on the falling water in case he was delayed.

You never know what might happen in a New River rice field.

Chapter Eleven
Mud and Megapixels

A bit farther to walk this time. A new moon coming and the flood tide had pushed water way up into the high marsh. Two in the afternoon, 90 degrees in the shade, no wind and the walking was slippery, sloppy and hard. Mud to his knees, sweat to his waist, he was wringing wet by the time he got to that gum tree.

But his camera was gone.

What the hell?

He sat on a pine log in dappled shade, lit a cigarette, pondered.

Somebody stole it, sure as shit! Somebody who don't want an endangered species effing up their development plans. Simmons, that fat-ass security guard? Maybe not Simmons himself, but likely one of his cohorts. Now what? Tracks, there had to be man tracks somewhere!

He eased to his feet, took a long look around. But that new moon flood had erased everything: no coon tracks, no deer tracks, no pig tracks. The only footprints were his own. He

Washed in the Blood

struck up the trail again. Maybe some man tracks beyond the tide line? He followed the canal along the edge of the field to where it hooked west at the foot of a long bluff. Fresh water up there, dark as strong coffee from rotting logs and leaves. He spotted a gator slide coming down from higher ground. But huge gator tracks were all he found.

It obviously was full grown; reptilian claws bigger than panther pugs, a belly bulge almost three feet across. Then Rut saw a thin lines of little bubbles rising in the dark water of the canal — two little trails, one from each nostril. Oh shit, too close. A gator is quicker than a deer for the first thirty feet, come at you in a sudden rush. Grab an arm or a leg, pull you under, drown your sorry ass quick. They don't have molars so they let you age a few days before they start gnawing. But by then it won't matter except to the coroner, the undertaker, your next of kin and maybe the neighbors downwind.

Rut pulled his revolver, hauled the hammer to full cock, eased back a dozen steps.

That's when he noticed a tattered canvas strap poking from the mud. It was the camera, half buried. *How in the hell did it get way back here?*

He retrieved the camera, wiped the worst of the mud onto his shirt.

Waterproof? It was designed to sit out in the rain, for weeks if needed. But who knows where the thing had been? This panther was getting expensive!

But Rut had absolutely no idea how expensive it would eventually be.

Jen was behind the bar and still in a huff when he arrived at Mudbank Mammy's. He drank Blue Point Toasted Lager or Red Stripe when he drank beer; Jim Beam bourbon when he wasn't. Gallons of both at Mammy's over the last ten months.

"And what would you like, sir?" She was damn pretty when she was mad, even prettier than usual this time. The air fairly crackled when she spoke.

"You know what I like."

"I thought I did," she said. "Oh yes, I remember now." She poured a weak shot of Beam, but when she reached for the mixer wand, she hit the wrong button on purpose, not water but Seven Up. It was clear, mostly clear anyway, with a slight green tint like island well water. He did not know the difference until he took a slug.

He spit a mouthful back into the glass. Some of it missed, ran down his chin, spattered onto the bar. "Damn, Jen!"

She grinned spitefully. "Oh, sorry! It's Beam and water, right?" Good thing she had no kerosene handy.

She sloshed his drink down the drain, ran a towel over the mess he made, poured another, water this time, still light on the Beam.

Rut dug the muddy camera out of his vest. The case was cracked and there were tooth marks all over it. He'd pulled off the battered strap and broken buckle. Now it was about the size of a pack of Camels. "Could you rinse the mud off this for me?"

Jen wrinkled her nose. "Where in the hell did you meet her?"

"Over a Ford tailgate," he said.

"What!"

"Come on, babe. Wash the mud off this."

Jen took it, turned it this way and that. "What is it?"

"Game camera."

"Where'd you get it?"

"Found it in the mud. Curious what's on it, that's all."

Jen rinsed it in the sink, dried it with a towel, laid it on the bar next to his drink, mostly gone now. She made him another, a fair measure this time. "You said you liked my hair," she said as she ran her hand over what little hair she had.

There was a little rubber hatch on the side of the camera, photo chip inside. Rut picked at it with his thumbnail. "Oh, but you know I do."

"Hers is clean down to her waist," she pouted.

Rut popped out the photo chip, slid it into his wallet. He pulled out a twenty, laid it on the bar. "She's a cop," he said.

"A cop?" Now she was spun up all over again. "Are you crazy? YOU bringing a cop down here?"

"Don't worry, babe. She was off-duty. I got her to smoke a joint."

"Off-duty? A cop is never off duty! Just don't bring her in here!"

"I won't, don't worry."

"And you'd better watch your ass!"

Jen didn't know even half of it.

Back at the shack, Rut mixed a drink, rolled a smoke while he waited for the computer to boot up, making a racket like marbles rolling around in a galvanized ten-quart pail. The moon was a delicate crescent low over the west, hardly visible in the peach-and-violet flush of the dying sun. The tide was rushing toward full flood and the Spanish moss moved on the river wind and the night birds cried. In the low scrub around his yard a few fireflies flickered. He remembered seeing them tangled in Callahan's hair while they both sat naked together in the cool wet grass, and how she insisted that he release each firefly unharmed and how he was happy to do as she wished.

He called up the Department of Natural Resources first, clicked on the Staff icon, then waded through all the *ologists:* biologists, herpetologists, ornithologists, archaeologists. OK, here we go, enforcement: Callahan, Charlotte. He did not know how to save her email, so he wrote it on the back of his power bill, now a week overdue. *charlotte.c@dnr.sc.gov.us*

He plugged the photocard into the reader and took a look: it was like the gangway to Noah's Ark. A coon, an otter, another coon, a four-foot gator, a wild hog's ass, and then … *What?*

The panther, the panther sure as shit!

Wait a minute. It was close, so close it was blurry. Just the face, inches from the lens: eyes, nose, ears. Then a shot of spartina grass when the cat peeled the camera clean off the tree. It had my scent on it! He knew I was there and he don't like it one damn bit!

It was fixing to get personal.

They ran them with hounds in the old days, shot them when they went to tree. He had lots of trees but no hounds of his own. Not for panthers anyway. Local hounds today are specialists.

Washed in the Blood

Some ranged close, others ranged far. Some ran deer but not hogs. Others ran hogs but not deer. Some ran coons and only coons — never rabbits, hogs or deer. But none ran panthers anymore as there were no panthers for twenty generations of hounds. Even if he could find some cat hounds, they would run bobcats. If he tried, they'd likely run his panther onto the high ground where the big cat could hold its own. And somebody would hear all the barking and screaming and call the law on him, which might mean the DNR, which might mean Callahan, and a fine mess that might be.

Thus, he decided, the panther must come to him. Bait and a blind might work. Like leopard bait in those old books about Africa, like he read about in Hemingway, Ruark and such when he was young. Rut was into his fourth whiskey now, counting the ones Jen had poured him earlier. His blood and courage were up. He'd hunted those rice fields half his life and still had all his fingers and toes, just a few scratches and bruises, but no serious leaks. He wouldn't use a deer for bait as deer season was many weeks away. He couldn't use a live goat, as a goat costs money, especially with the Jamaicans buying them up for barbeque the way they were. They'd take the rankest billy goat, feed him a pint of whiskey, wrestle him down and push a field pea down one of its ears. The billy would run 'round in circles all day long, trying to shake that pea loose, and by sundown, he'd taste as good as the finest lamb. That's what they said, anyway.

But it's always open season on wild hogs. He decided to knock off a young one, no more than forty pounds, easy dragging. He'd lay its scent trail up and down that canal and wire the hog up into that same oak where he saw the ragged remains of the buck fawn. Hell, he'd even wrap the pig in his sweaty T-shirt and lay down his own scent too now he knew from what was left of the camera that the panther held a grudge.

The next bourbon tasted especially good!

He sent the cat-face picture to Callahan and it was almost a week before he got a reply. Not from Callahan, rather the same assistant biologist for endangered species who dismissed his initial report: Jerry Drinkwater.

Dear Mr. Elliott, Officer Callahan forwarded your recent email to me for my response. Your attached game camera photo appears to show a bobcat, which are quite common in the area you mention. However, your photo does not have a date or time imprint. Make sure you set up your camera to include day, time and GPS coordinates if it has such a feature. Thank you for your continuing interest in South Carolina wildlife.

Suck-egg bastard!

What's it gonna take?

He'd kill that pig and set that bait and build a blind and sit in it till he got a photo. He had an old Pentax camera and you could still find film if you weren't fussy about black and white or color or film speed. Just push the button, get a picture, pure and simple. He'd make a sign and nail it to the tree. No way to record the time, but he would write the date and place with an indelible marker, let the bastards try and deny that.

But he couldn't raise Callahan. He called her. She didn't answer. He left no message but he reckoned her cell phone noted his number. Some women get scarce if they think maybe they like you too much. Which was a good thing to think, even if it was wrong.

Chapter Twelve

Behold the Earth and the Bounty Thereof

Before Rut could indulge himself with panthers or women, there was a most immediate concern: his budding crop of marijuana and picking, hanging and drying thereof. The plants were up over the sweet corn and about to top the sunflowers, with blossoms big as hubcaps. Rut didn't pick reefer by the day of the month or by the phase of the moon. He picked it when other folks could spot it.

Wire cutters worked best.

For the first cutting, he snipped the whirls and knots of tight little leaves at the ends of major branches as big as old-fashioned, U.S. Army-issued, D-cell flashlights. Clipping the tops of the plants hides them again amongst the sweet corn and sunflowers.

Rut gathered the early growth in threes and fours, tied them together in bundles with hanks of sisal baling twine and hung each upside down from nails driven into his chicken-coop rafters. Good reefer smells like an aggravated skunk. The aroma of chicken manure helps cover the distinct stench of pot somewhat. He hung each bundle upside down so what little sap was in the stems, which you couldn't smoke, would wind down into the leaf balls, which you could. It was a fair to middling crop this year: Six or seven pounds when dry.

Meanwhile, the female plants, suddenly stripped of their sexuality, go ballistic, breaking out all over with smaller, more numerous and more potent buds. They would be ready in a month or so, but too small for bundling and hanging like the first cutting. These are laid an inch deep in the bottoms of paper Piggly Wiggly shopping bags, left open. Winn-Dixie bags would work in a pinch although the buds are so heavy with oil that they seem wet even when dry.

Ten grand in a good year covers taxes, insurance and the light bill. Like a man drawing Social Security, it isn't a living, but it does take the edge off poverty. But if a man has reefer, he does have lots of friends.

Rut didn't mess with the stems and low-grade leaf, as they could result in legal entanglements equal to the finest buds. One year he deep-fried a gallon of leaves and such in peanut oil, like frying a turkey. He strained it carefully and used the dark green oil for making brownies. But only once. Way too potent. Smoking it was safer — you could stop when you wanted to. Once you ate it, you could not un-eat it. You were toast. So Rut ran the considerable leftovers through a garden mulcher after the second picking and tilled it back into the soil. Sandy island ground needed all the help it could get.

Ah, the bounty of the earth. Callahan met him at the Red Roof Inn in Hardeeville. This was right after he picked up a fifty-pound sack of cob corn from Pritchardville Feed and Seed. Grain corn is fine for high-ground hogs but cob corn makes the best bait in the mud. Wild hogs stomp and roll the cobs in the mud, then root them up again. Keeps them busy, on the bait longer.

It was late afternoon, still blazing hot, and he waited in the shade from the Huddle House sign slanting across the motel parking lot, the truck idling and the AC on max. Damn poor weather to even be thinking about killing a pig, even if it was not really pork he was after. Callahan pulled off the freeway, stopped at the Circle K for gas. She was in uniform and armed, in a government truck, four-wheel-drive, dark green with SCDNR Enforcement on each door. His heart ached as he watched her from a distance. My God, what a beauty.

He was toast and by now he knew it.

She topped off her fuel tank, locked the truck, went into the store. He was waiting when she came back with a pack of Nabs and a bottled water. He rolled his window down. "I'm sorry ma'am. I forgot to bring the fireflies."

She smiled. "You can be my firefly."

He chose a long marshy point on the Jasper County side of the river. There was a deep winding creek to hide the boat. The

Washed in the Blood

bottom of the creek was hard sand and easy walking at low tide. The creekbanks were as soft as grandma's chocolate pudding, but once up on the flat, walking was easy again. And then there was the wind, prevailing out of the southwest this time of year. Low tide, he'd be sneaking upwind, perfect. On a daybreak high tide the wind did not matter so much. He could shoot right out of the boat, single-ought buckshot has long reach. Old timers called them "blue whistlers" for a reason.

Rut went in on the late morning high tide, halfway through the moon. He was hauling a six-gallon bucket of cob corn and thinking about Callahan and the little wet spot on her game warden britches when she walked out of the Red Roof door at dawn. Watch out boy! A man best keep his mind on business while messing with panthers, rattlesnakes, moccasins, hogs, gators and maybe bears, if Capum Pete wasn't bullshitting him.

He ran the bow of the skiff up into the marsh, worked an oar into the mud, secured the boat with a loop of dock line. He slogged ashore and tossed half the cobs underhanded in a twenty-foot radius. He'd give the pigs a few days to find it, then throw down the rest of the corn. Third trip, he'd slip in at first light with buckshot.

By the time he got the pig hauled to that rice canal, up in the live oak and wired to a limb, by the time he got his blind built, it would be a hellish long and hot day. Five, six round trips at forty miles each, he could have crossed the Florida Straits from Homestead to Bimini with the fuel he was fixing to burn. All for a picture of a panther, a critter that did not exist?

Rut was coming unwrapped. Seriously unwrapped.

He just got paid for a fat job, a government job, hard to come by these days: building a sand fence to stabilize a bird island in the Savannah channel. The Georgia Department of Transportation had to build it, mitigation for marshes they filled to four-lane a state highway down in McIntosh County. Coyotes, coons and armadillos were raising hell with ground-nesting seabirds all up and down the lower Savannah and a sand island they could not get to seemed a good idea.

But some bad McIntosh mud mojo must have followed the money. Gales leveled the sand piles and storm tides overtopped them and the whole God's thing was about to wash away. Shallow water on all sides, it was a perfect job for a landing craft, and Rut had one. He put over a hundred rolls of fence ashore, to be strung later by convicts in Georgia's Sentenced to Serve program. Easy duty for the guards; nowhere to run, nowhere to hide for the prisoners. It was a three-acre sand island two miles from shore.

Money in his pocket, Rut hollered up Jimmie Jenkins. Jimmie had a new job, now that he finally got his license back, driving for a transportation company over on Hilton Head. "Hey Jimmie, how you do?"

"Jus' fine, Mister Rut, how 'bout you?"

"Doin' OK. Can I get that limo for a couple hours?"

Long pause. "Mister Rut, my boss get two hundred dollar an hour fo' dat limo. What you want 'em fo'? Trying to shake loose some pussy? Boss get fifty extry fo' de clean up."

"You know me my whole life," Rut said. "You know I don't need no car for to get pussy."

Jimmie chuckled. "Dat sho' is right. You got boat fo' dat."

"Look here. How much your boss get for that limo?"

"I done tole you. Two hundred a hour."

"I know, but how much you get?"

"We split 'em fifty-fifty."

"OK. I give you two hundred fo' two hours fo' yo' boss and a ounce of good reefer fo' you. How dat sound?"

Another chuckle. "Mister Rut, you and me is talking now."

Jimmie picked him up at All Joy and waited while he ducked into the Tanger Outlet Mall on U.S. 278. Anything Tanger sold, you could likely get cheaper someplace else but the tourists all think they're getting deals straight from the factory. Rut didn't mind so much that day. He was on a mission and at one hundred bucks an hour, he had no time to go wading around Target. He came back to the limo in a Tommy Bahama white shirt, a pair of pink Ralph Lauren Bermuda shorts, a Chinese imitation alligator skin belt and Chinese imitation Bass loafers, no socks.

Jimmie eyed him up and down, sadly shook his head. "I don't know who you tryin' to fool, Mister Rut, but it ain't gone work."

"Why not?" Rut asked.

"Yo' feets too white," Jimmie said.

The real estate office at Palmetto Bluff was two double-wide trailers bolted together, a gracious Southern porch façade tacked on front, rocking chairs and potted hibiscus and a ficus tree from Home Depot, and by the door, an outside ashtray full of cat litter and expensive cigar butts. Rut played the rules this time. Played them, not by them.

Jimmie, in his white shirt, black tie and chauffeur cap, breezed him right through the gate, pulled up before the real estate office, got out and opened his door. "Jimmie, if I could afford you, I'd never drive again."

Jimmie patted his shirt pocket. "If you keep slipping me dis, you wouldn't haff to walk or drive."

"I'll be quick as I can."

"Take yo' time, Mister Rut, jus' don't bullshit 'em too hard."

Pretty brunette behind the desk, nice dress, high heels, jewelry from Tanger Outlet. Audubon bird prints and maps all over the walls. Some of the maps were old ones, reproductions of the 1825 Mills Atlas and such. Others were new: what the place would look like built out.

"Good afternoon," she said. "Can I help you, sir?"

She rose and took his hand. She told him her name but he promptly forgot it.

"My name is Elliott," he said. "The wife and I came down from Atlanta, looking to relocate on the coast." He told her the same lie he told the security guard. "I was born and raised just up the road. Trying to get back home, you know how that is."

"Oh yes," she said, "I am from Cleveland. It used to be such a pretty town. I notice you have a driver."

"Sorry," Rut said. If lies made your tongue swell, his would have swole up, turned black and splattered on the floor like a rotten deer liver. He was right proud of himself: "He's on salary. Might as well let him drive." The girl did not see the South Carolina commercial plates, good thing.

"And what sort of business are you in, Mr. …?"

"Elliott," he said.

"Yes, Mr. Elliott."

"Steel," he said, "tube steel." He paused, "Tapered tube steel. You see all those billboards along I-16?"

"Yes," she said, "of course."

"That's my steel."

"Well, sir, please have a seat." She motioned to a chair at a coffee table. Copies of *Southern Living*, and *Coastal Living*, and an antique mallard decoy on top of them. "I'll call one of our sales associates."

Which she did.

Chapter Thirteen

Visions and Dreams

Traffic was stacking up on U.S. 278, Ohio and New York plates mostly, timeshare and condo turnover time on Hilton Head Island. There was a liquor store on the right. "Pull over," Rut said.

Rut came back with two pints of Jim Beam, the King James Version, he called it.

One for him, the other for Jimmie.

"Dis wash de green down real good," Jimmie said.

Jimmie dropped him off at All Joy Landing, but before they parted, they opened their bottles, clinked them together in a toast before taking a generous slug.

"To the woods," Rut said.

Jimmie drank first, his eyes teared up and he smacked his lips. "To de green!" he replied.

Off the clock and out of sight, Rut opened his own door this time. "I love you my brother."

"I love you mo'," Jimmie hiccupped. "Jesus take the wheel."

Rut shucked his store-bought clothes, slipped over the stern and briefly swam naked in the May River salt. Clean again, he put on his old clothes, stuffed the new duds into the chart locker, fired the skiff, backed away from the pier and idled downriver in the no-wake zone around the rich folks' docks, the little fire of the King James burning in his belly.

He was thinking back on his subterfuge with considerable satisfaction. That girl fetched up a man from a back office who laid out the grand vision for Palmetto Bluff. They had permits for twenty thousand homes but were committed to dropping density to only two thousand. They were building a golf course and a marina and a perfect movie set village on the water, brick streets and genuine gas streetlights. A boutique hotel, rental cottages, a general store, even a chapel. Electric vehicles were encouraged but not required except it would be electric boats only in a seven-mile network of interior canals. Town lots started around $200,000 and ten-acre estate lots along the May River started at $2 million. Rut strode over to the large-scale master map, as big as a sheet of plywood. He eyed it briefly, then put his finger on the high ground nearest to where he found his shattered game camera. "Here," he said, "how about something here?"

Between the vision and revision falls the shadow. Sophomore English at Carolina came rushing back now and then, mostly when least expected.

Hemming and hawing, the clearing of throats, a quick glance between the receptionist and the real estate wonk. "Ah,

Mr. Elliott, that is slated for future development."

"That's fine," Rut said, "You can sell me five acres right now. I can get you half the cash by this time tomorrow. Other half when you get me access and a survey. I wasn't planning on building right away."

Another long pause.

"I'm sorry, we just can't do that. There are still environmental assessments to be done."

Environment assessments! Oh, my aching ass! Did they know about the panther too? He thought.

They loaded him up with smaller maps and sundry artist's conceptual promotional material, but he had left all of it in the limo. Didn't matter. He was not going back, not through the front gate anyway.

When Jesus quit the carpenter trade to take up preaching full time, He went out into the wilderness for forty days. The devil came to Him one afternoon when He was hungry. "You the Son of God? Turn these rocks into bread and make a tomato sandwich."

And Jesus said, "Man can't live by bread alone."

And then the devil took Him to a high cliff and said, "Hey man, you the Chosen One. Your coming was ordained before the creation of the world. Don't waste it. Jump, the angels will bear you up lest you even cut your foot on an oyster shell." Actually, it was "dash your foot against a stone." But there were no stones where Rut lived.

Washed in the Blood

And Jesus said to the devil, "Don't you know your scriptures? It says do not tempt God!"

And as long as they were up there, the devil waved his hands and Jesus could see all the great cities of the world: New York, Babylon and Savannah. "I'll give You all of this if you just work for me instead of God."

Jesus must have liked cities about as much as Rut did. "Get behind me, Satan!" he said.

And the devil left Him and pestered Him no more.

Rut had been tempting God alright. Now it was Sunday morning, time for some serious churching, long overdue.

The deacon met him at the church-house door. Baptists preach that the church is the whole body of believers, not the building. The building is the church-house, that which houses the people, which are the church.

"Welcome, Brother Elliott, we ain't seen you in a spell."

They shook hands.

"I been mighty busy," Rut said.

"You might be too busy fo' Jekus, but Jekus ain't never too busy fo' you."

"I know that, Deke. I do better next time."

"I knows you will, brother, I knows you will."

The church-house had two doors, one on the right for the women to come and go, one on the left for the men. The pews were divided down the middle with a board bulkhead. Women on the right, men on the left. There was no choir loft; there was no choir. Everybody could sing. Rut sat in the last pew, close to the door. That way he could slip out without any undo commotion.

The preacher was not a local. He came over from Alabammy — was a dentist and a ladies' man in his former life. Then he had a brain tumor that left him blind. They cut the entire top of his skull loose, snaked out the tumor and he got his sight back. He reckoned he was like Saul of Tarsus, struck blind on the road to Damascus for his wicked ways. He got religion, abandoned his dental practice and went off to seminary at age sixty. He still had an eye for the girls but he kept his britches up, so far as anybody knew.

He wore a bright yellow silk suit that Sunday with patent leather iridescent green shoes. From a distance he looked like an underripe banana stood end. Up close he boomed like an Old Testament prophet, and his sermons often recalled his former wickedness — to Rut's considerable delight.

But first, came the deacon's prayer, which always began and ended the same, the minutes between were always different and often interminable, lines and couplets from old-time spirituals strung together as he was moved by the spirit. Most folks knew better than to ask the deacon for a table grace, lest the gravy set up and the rice petrify.

"Amazing sight the Savior stands, he knocks at every do';

Ten thousand blessings in each hand to satisfy the po';

Almighty everlasting God, look down on us as we pray…."

Then he'd rock back on his heels, look up like he was reading a script off the old beadboard ceiling. Ten minutes into it, you'd know he was winding it up when he'd pray: "An when You swing low in Yo' sweet chariot, don't You leave without ol' Deke aboard, and give us a home, Lord, give us a home…" He was wailing now "in that sacred space where Jesus are, amen."

And then he'd break into song, "Gonna Trust in the Lord till I Die."

Washed in the Blood

The sermon that day was from the Prophet Joel, a minor Old Testament preacher. Everybody brought their Bibles to church and there were extra in each pew in case you forgot yours. That way, every time the preacher quoted the Book, he'd quote chapter and verse so you could look it up and know the preacher wasn't just talking out of his head.

The preacher mounted the pulpit and faced the church, the body of believers. No holy decorations in a Baptist church-house, no plaster saints, no candles, not even an altar, just a crude wooden cross on the wall that used to sit atop of old Praise House, the slave chapel lost to a hurricane wind so many years before. "I want you to turn to the Book of Joel, second chapter, verse two."

There was a rustling of paper, the flipping of pages. Some of the Bibles were beat all to hell, covers patched with masking, Scotch, even duct tape, many pages with verses underlined and notes in pencil in the margins. Owners of the most worn books found Joel quicker than the rest.

"Daniel, Hosea, Joel," the preacher coached.

Even though the Lord had brought him back from blindness, his vision was not the best. He slipped on a pair of reading glasses and traced the line with his forefinger as he read: "Blow a trumpet on Zion, and sound an alarm on my Holy mountain! Let all the inhabitants of the land tremble, for the Day of the Lord is coming; surely it is near."

Then he read it again. "For the Day of the Lord is coming, surely it is near!"

He let that sink in, then said, "This was after the division of Israel, and Joel lived in the southern half, the Kingdom of Judea. The people were sinning and straying, a-whoring after strange gods."

"Amen!" a woman hollered. "Thank you, Jesus!"

"And thank you sister!" the preacher said. "God sent plagues of locusts to eat up the crops. Three plagues, and when the last locusts were done, there was famine in the land. Not even fodder for the cattle and sheep!"

He looked out among the faithful. "And what gods are you a-whoring after? You know in Joel's day, some people had fallen away from Jehovah God and were worshipping Baal! God set them free in Egypt-land, parted the sea for their freedom, led them though the wilderness, a cloud by day and a pillar of fire by night, gave them a land of milk and honey but they forgot! They forgot and they worshipped Baal!"

"Oh no!" a man shouted.

"Oh yes!" the preacher replied. "And the Baal church was nothing more than a brothel, a whorehouse! That's how you worshiped Baal! You have sex with a priestess and you leave money in the collection plate!"

"Great God!" somebody else hollered. Rut could not tell if it was a shout of dismay or approval.

"Now what kind of gods are WE a-whoring after? What do YOU put before Jehovah God? You want a fancy car with whitewall tires and lots of chrome? You gamble? You drink that likker till you feel so bad you can't get to the church-house? What you put before God? That's the god you are a-whoring after!"

Quick glances among the faithful. *He ain't talkin' bout me? He talkin' bout you! Who he talkin' bout anyway?*

"Brothers and sisters," the preacher continued after a long pause, "turn to Proverbs 5.3."

Rut found it quick enough.

"You know when Jesus read Scripture at the synagogue in His hometown, he stood before he read, so brother Elliott, could you please stand and read that for us?"

Oh shit! I'm busted, Rut thought.

He stood, cleared his throat. "The lips of a strange woman drip honey, yea, her voice is smoother than oil."

"Thank you, Brother Rutledge. But keep standing, I'm not done with you yet."

Several sisters swiveled in their pews, nodded, cast knowing eyes and sly smiles.

"But God is merciful above all things if we just humble ourselves before Him. Now Brother Elliott, you still got your finger in the Book of Joel?"

Rut did.

"Can you read us 2.23?"

Rut cleared his throat again as his heart hammered in his chest. "And it shall come to pass afterward, *that* I will pour out my spirit upon all flesh; and your sons and your daughters shall prophesy, your old men shall dream dreams, your young men shall see visions."

"Thank you, brother, you may sit down now. You have a strong voice and we will call upon you again."

The preacher did not say, "as soon as you get your back-sliding ass back in the church-house" but everybody knew what he meant. Back-sliding was bad, the worst there was, willingly turning your back on the Holy Spirit. The Spirit was the Hound of Heaven, on your trail day and night. You'd be wise to chum that Hound, feed him and love him or he would give you no rest. Dog being God spelled backward the way it is.

Rut figured to get a pup soon as things calmed down a bit, if they ever would. A bitch lab and he would call her Mojo, after that old Gullah stump-hole magic, and she would be magic indeed, but a man best not think about that when Washed in the Blood.

Then the preacher turned to Miss Evonne. "Sister, can you give us a song?"

The preacher wasn't a local. If he had been, he would have said, "Please, sister, give us a song," as he would have known all the Gullah sisters could sing.

Most times Miss Evonne would offer that simple hymn from her childhood — "Jesus loves me, this I know …" — sometimes seated and at times barely louder than a whisper. But this time she stood, threw back her head and bellered while her face beaded up and ran with sweat:

"I got a home in dat rock, don't you see,

I got a home in dat rock, don't you see,

Jus' between de earth an' sky,

Where my po' Jekus bleed an' die

I got a home in dat rock, don't you see."

Rut knew the song well. It came from the days before hymnals, indeed in the days before most Gullah could read or write, simple repletion of lines, easy to remember. Then another verse Rut had never heard, but it filled his heart to overflowing:

"I got a home at las', don't you see.

I got a home at las'

I got a home in de tall marsh grass,

I got a home in dat rock."

Chapter Fourteen

Fire and Ice

Rut hit the river at sunrise on a new moon flood tide. Flood tide at his dock at least. The New River was so cussedly crooked, the tides were almost backward in its headwaters. Halfway up at the spot where he left the pig bait, it was half tide and rising, nowhere near full. He'd ride the flood tide up, lay down more corn, ride the ebb tide home, a good plan. Halfway to the dock, he turned his pickup around. He knew he'd score a pig. He always did. Why not go ahead and build the blind? He let truck idle while he rooted around in the toolshed. Machete, handsaw, bush-hook. Yes, but he'd leave the chainsaw. Too much racket. Nobody would know what he was up to from now on, not Palmetto Bluff Security, not Yancey, not even Callahan.

The river was as lovely as always as he buzzed around the switchback turns and then idled up that little creek on the Jasper County side. Late summer now, the marsh grass had lost the springtime green, fading to brown and soon to be lit with the fires of autumn, gold as grain ready for the harvest. Tide was high enough by then to nose the skiff up into the high marsh and step ashore onto almost dry ground. The pigs had found the bait like he knew they would. The spartina canes were knocked over, the mud churned up and only a few grains of corn remained. He threw down the last bucket of cobs, dumped the last loose grains remaining, rattled the bucket so the pigs would hear it, then got back into the skiff, blubbered back down the creek and headed upriver to the rice canal.

It was the same as he last saw it. He grabbed his pistol, his bushhook and handsaw and walked the trail. He found no new tracks excepting either hogs or deer — hard to tell the difference sometimes, especially after a couple of high tides and a rain. He wanted the morning sun at his back, twenty yards to the east was a low hillock sprouting a few pine saplings and some sizable wax myrtle and black ti-ti bushes. He cleared a shooting lane between the hillock and the live oak, not for a bullet or a charge of buckshot, but for the photo from the old Pentax. He gathered the bush trimmings, stuck the biggest in the ground in a semicircle, then wove the smaller pieces horizontally in between. In an hour it would have served as a duck blind had it been on the edge of the water instead of deep in the woods along an old rice dike. The chore completed to his satisfaction, he turned the bait bucket upside down — something to sit on, perfect — then made his way back to the boat.

Tide was still flooding almost full now and he idled along, just fast enough so the boat would answer the helm. He worked the wheel this way and that to keep to the middle of the canal. *Grunt, grunt,* the engine was mounted in rubber bushings that complained, *grunt, grunt.* He was lighting a cigarette when there came a sudden scramble out in the marsh and a pig rushed the edge of the canal, parting the canes, laying a wake like an oncoming torpedo. He dropped the smoke, thankfully overboard and not in the bilge, and grabbed his revolver. *Fixing to get my bait pig right here and now,* he thought.

But no. Once the pig heard the murmur of the outboard and the hissing of the boat wake, it changed its mind, and at the last second refused to show. Pistol out and hammer back, pulse in overdrive, there was nothing to shoot. But it gave Rut an idea. He had a hog call back at the shack, and was he pretty fluent with it. Once he got that bait hung in the tree, he'd grunt up that panther for his photo shoot.

Damn he was smart. It was all going according to plan.

Down at Mudbank Mammy's again, Jen looking fine as ever. The oaks were dropping acorns this time of year and the vets twitched each time one hit the roof, rattled down the tin and plooped into the azaleas beneath the eaves. "Incoming," somebody said, beer dripping down his chin.

Capum Pete was hooked over the end of the bar. Rut took the stool next to him. "Hey, Sonny, you find that bear yet?"

"Panther, Cap, not a bear. Mammy let you back in here?

"Yeah, but I'm on my best behavior." Pete raised his glass. "I dis-remember the details, either a panther or a hippo."

Jen brought him his whiskey. She gave it a swirl with her little finger, held it for him to lick. He did, tickling her fingertip with his tongue. He couldn't help himself. She didn't seem to mind.

"Cap, you got a block-and-tackle I can borry?"

Pete took a long pull on his beer. "Lem'me think."

"You must'a had something to hoist those drums of crabs."

"What you planning on lifting?

"Hog," Rut said.

Pete shook his head. "What's wrong with you, Sonny? You know it's too early to be butchering a pig!"

Jen brought him another drink. "This one's on me," she said.

The drink was long on whiskey but short on cubes. His almost-degree in English ambushed him again. He waved his glass in the air and said:

Some say the world will end in fire,

Some say in ice.

From what I've tasted of desire

I hold with those who favor fire.

But if it had to perish twice,

I think I know enough of hate

To say that for destruction ice

Is also great

And would suffice.

Jen shook her head. "You're crazy."

"The boy's been churchin' again," Capum Pete cackled. "He's done busted loose in unknown tongues."

Another acorn on the roof.

"Incoming," from one of the vets.

᛫

Four in the morning on a rising tide. A crooked river seems a lot crookeder in the dark. Generally keep to the outside of each turn, as the water is generally deeper there, but not always. In the rare straight stretches, shoal water could be anywhere. Over the years Rut must have hit them all, but each only once. Running a big skiff aground at speed is briefly terrifying and leaves an indelible mark on a man's memory, even if no damage is done. The skyglow from Savannah bounced off an overcast sky and lit up the river so he could run without lights, only his red and green bow lights in the off-chance he encountered traffic coming downriver. But there was no reason for anybody to be out at such an hour, unless tending a still or running dope. Not much reefer smuggling these days, America producing more than it could ever smoke. Lots of cocaine, though, but it mostly came in hidden in container freight bound for Savannah or via small boats from the Bahamas into south Florida, then by truck up I-95 to the big Yankee cities. Heroin? Likely from Mexico into San Diego. There was one crabber working this river, but not till sunup.

Rut's little creek was easy to spot, even in the dark. He throttled back and eased in with the tide, the engine no louder than a whisper. He knew the pigs would hear it but they'd be happily thinking he was bringing them breakfast like before. But this time, it was buckshot, not corn. He ran the skiff up into the marsh as usual, rattled the pail, uttered a few tentative grunts on his hog call, sat and waited for shooting light.

Daybreak comes sneaky beneath an overcast sky, no stars to fade, no East to streak up, a freshening breeze is your first clue. A thousand miles out to sea it was already morning and the sunlight was warming the water and moving the air. A soft grunt way off in the distance, Rut answered, and at once the bait was awash with pigs of various sizes, no more than ghostly shapes in the half-light of dawn. He eased his shotgun to his shoulder, picked out a smallish pig. But when he snicked the safety, the pigs erupted with a great collective snort and in an instant all of them were gone,

Washed in the Blood

like the canes and mud had swallowed them up. Twenty seconds, thirty, he coaxed them back with *a-hunka, a-hunka.*

A young pig was the first back in, still too dark to sex it, but Rut could see it turn its piggy head this way and that, seeking the source of that mysterious metallic click. Pigs are smart, the suck of mud or the snap of a twig would have never alarmed them, but metal on metal was the crack of doom. They have ear and nose to shame a blue-tick coon hound. Rut put the shotgun bead on a front shoulder, pulled the trigger and was briefly blinded by the muzzle flash. He never felt the recoil, never heard the report. He never did when pulling down on buck, boar or any other living thing. He damn near shot a man once, but didn't, Praise Jesus. The cops found him chest up in a watery ditch on Hilton Head some weeks later. The investigation was short and concise: "Natural causes," the coroner said, and he was entirely correct. Owing his crack dealer money was hard on his health, naturally.

Rut found the pig right where he shot it. It was a young boar, forty pounds, perfect. Front shoulders a bloody mess, buckshot having no mercy. The hams were perfect, backstraps too, maybe too good for a panther? Rut looped the carcass into the skiff, *splat.*

Rut was good with a blade and he knew this: you skin a pig from the inside out. Mud plastered on the hide will dull the finest steel quick. He made a tiny cut at the base of the skull, turned the knife over and ran it down the backbone to the base of the tail and pulled out the loins, quicker than it takes to tell you. He threw them in the cooler with his beer. He was on a roll since Palmetto Bluff — Yankee beer, Blue Point. Hams and guts for the panther. Panthers liked guts, he reckoned after feral cats got into his chickens.

Half hour later, it was broad daylight, *day-clean,* the Gullah say, and he was back in that rice canal where all his trouble started.

Tide still flooding, he dropped his anchor off his stern to keep from getting hung up beneath the deadfall pine blocking further progress up the canal. He wrestled what was left of his pig ashore, but before hoisting it into the live oak, he rigged a rope around its neck and drug it up and down the game trail to lay a scent.

There was one final ruse in Rut's bag of many tricks, a tiny vial of bobcat urine. He knew big cats are solitary and territorial, sociable only during breeding season. As it takes about one hundred square miles of range to satisfy a tom, about three-quarters of that for a female, he figured to dope his bait with panther piss. He searched long and hard on the internet one bleary evening but the only thing he found was a spray like Knocker-Loose or WD-40 to lubricate rusty nuts and bolts. But there was bobcat urine listed on a trapper's supply site. A one-ounce bottle for twenty bucks. He didn't mind much as he was so far into the mission at that point, twenty bucks was chump change. The bottle came with a little wick to disperse the scent, but he used a wad of Spanish moss instead and saved some for later.

He was back home by likker-thirty, cocktail time. He'd give his set a week or so, then come back with shotgun and camera.

Rut called it a good day.

Chapter Fifteen

When the Devil Beat His Wife Behind the Door

The storm came ashore as a Category One, about halfway between Biloxi and Mobile. It roared up the Mississippi Valley, broke up crossing the Great Blue Ridge and fell upon them from behind as a vicious line of thunder-squalls all crackling blue fire. That kept Rut off the river four days longer than he intended, and left him with a gnarly old pine across his driveway he had to cut before he could get to the dock. Third day was a ragged sky and intermittent rain and on the fourth it sometimes rained when the sun was shining, a sure sign the Gullah say: "That ol' Debil be beatin' he wife behind de doe'."

The saying raised some serious theological questions, best considered on the front porch with a beer and a reefer while the tide brimmed, fluttered and fell. Was the devil married? Did he engage in domestic violence? And lastly, did hell have a door?

First two questions remained a mystery but the last was easy, as there was a time-worn line appropriate to late summer in these parts, "It's hotter than the hinges of hell." So, if hell had hinges, it must have a door!

Case closed.

Rut fired another joint and wondered what Callahan was up to right then. He wobbled inside and gave her a call.

No answer.

He was drifting off to blue ocean dreams when his phone popped off. "I got my eye on you boy," she said.

"Where you?" His voice was husky with sleep.

"At the end of your driveway," she said. "Infrared."

"Great God-amighty! Come on up!"

"Get naked and I can find you in the dark."

"I'm naked as a jay, can't you see that?"

She laughed. "I'm on stake-out on John's Island. Just fooling."

"Who you watching?"

"Night hunters," she said.

"For God's sake be careful! Them crack-head sons-of-bitches shoot!"

"I got on my flak jacket," she said, "but it's a little snug around my belly."

"What!"

The line went dead.

Another wee-hour trip up New River. He knew it well by then, in daylight and dark. If this kept up, someday he might know it as well as Capum Pete. But Capum Pete had no reason to run it at night. Rut didn't either, except those "no panther" emails from the Department of Natural Resources, each one like burning fat-lighter stick drove up his butt — damn them, damn them to hell. Rut had never seen the panther but Yancey had, and Yancey's word was good as gold unless he owed you money for dope.

Call me a liar? Rut fumed to himself.

Of course, the DNR never called him a liar. A cop might call you a liar during interrogation but never would an assistant biologist for endangered species do so — way too polite for that. Instead, the message was that Rut was mistaken, deluded, hallucinating. Even Callahan, who very likely loved him by now, thought he was a fool. Rut guessed Palmetto Bluff knew about the beast but was keeping mum. *Can't blame them for that, as it didn't really exist,* Rut thought. *OK, time to stop thinking about all that.* His rice canal was coming up fast.

He idled along in the half-light, one eye peeled for floating wreckage of the old Seaboard Airline Railway trestle, or Sherman's pontoon bridge like Yancey said. Didn't matter which if you ran into it. Past that hazard, he secured the skiff, gathered his shotgun, camera, flashlight and stepped ashore into a great cloud of mosquitoes.

There are fifty-six separate species hereabout, some say fifty-seven. A few transmit deadly diseases but the most pestiferous, the Salt Marsh Mosquito, does not. Good thing, as neither county, state or the Feds will allow spraying over tidal marshes. You just got to tough it out. Rut always wore a broad-brimmed hat with a net he could pull down over his face. The bugs would roost along the edge of the brim, a dozen at a time like buzzards in a pine, contemplating how to get through the mesh. If there is a hole no bigger than a match-head, they'd find it.

He eased to the live oak, played the light among the branches. The bait had been hit, alright, guts gone and only a half a ham remaining. He dosed the base of the tree with another shot of bobcat urine, got some of it on his fingers. Nasty stuff, strong as household ammonia. He wiped his fingers on a pants-leg and dropped the empty vial on the ground.

In his blind, he set his old Pentax lens to a five-point-six and the shutter speed to one-hundred and twenty-fifths of a second, good for most any situation. The tail, he had to get a picture of that tail. He blew a series of soft grunt on his hog-call, settled in to wait on daybreak.

Ten minutes, fifteen, another series of grunts when something hit him across the broad of his back like a baseball bat. He heard the roar of his shotgun as his world faded to black.

The sun was halfway up the sky when he regained consciousness, the blood running down his right arm was crusted and dry and the blow-flies had found it. He sat up, then stood as the swamp and woods reeled around him. He tried to remember where he was. It came back in bits and pieces. *Knocked cold for two hours, maybe three? Jesus!* Lucky the pigs or gators hadn't eaten him alive. Where was his camera? His neck muscles were as tight and twisted as manila rope. *Whiplash?* His hands shook as he struggled to light a cigarette. Backs of his hands so swollen from mosquito bites he could see neither vein or bone.

His shotgun was half buried in leaves and mud, the fired shell still in the chamber. He retrieved it, jacked a fresh round into the battery. His shoulder hurt and his right sleeve was almost torn clean off his shirt. He reckoned he was still bleeding back there but no way he could see it.

What the hell happened, anyway?

Then he saw it — a black paw protruding from the scrub on the far side of the live oak. He was shaking from shock before but now he shook with rage. That big bastard mistook him for a hog? Maybe for a bobcat from the piss he rubbed on his britches? What a dumbass he was! He couldn't be sure, but he suddenly knew what he was going to do. He knew what he had to do. The skiff was full of fuel and the day was yet young. He would haul that panther to the DNR in Port Royal, by God! He'd dump it on their office steps like he told Callahan he'd do!

The load of buckshot had caught the cat just beneath the tail and there was not enough anatomy left for him to determine the gender. *Likely a tom from its size, nearly two-hundred pounds*. He got a rope around its neck and began the long drag to the boat, his anger lightening his load and dulling his pain. God, what a beautiful animal! He was sorry he killed it. He must have killed it, even if he did not remember and never would. The fire was long gone from its yellow eyes by the time he found it, good thing. That would have haunted him forever.

The trip down New River, across the sound and up to Port Royal was a blur. He hailed the marina on his VHF, channel sixteen, switched to sixty-eight as requested. He asked for assistance at the fuel dock, a man and a dock cart and Desmond were waiting when he idled up to the float.

"Oh, Meester Rut, you hurt yourself!" And then Desmond

saw the cat, stretched out on the deck behind the steering station, and his eyes got big as Oreos. "Oh no, Meester Rut, what you do! You keel dis cat, mon?"

Rut gritted his teeth. "Gim'me a hand with this thing." He drug the carcass to the edge of the skiff and with a single mighty heave, threw it upon the dock. It left a broad smear of blood across the deck and dock boards.

"What you do now, Meester Rut?"

"I'm gon'na haul it up to the DNR!"

This threw Desmond into a high panic. "Oh no, Meester Rut, you cannot do dis! I told you, stay clear of dem blood clot! You leave dis cat with me. I cut him up for de crab trap," he put three fingers to his lips made a kissing sound, "*poof* — he gone." And then he added, "We keel small cat round here, de crab eats 'em up jus' fine."

Turn feral cats into blue crab meat, a good deal if you don't ponder the details. Two hundred pounds of panther would make a ton of crab. Feral cats on the docks, they ate wharf rats, mice, birds, garbage. But since the iguanas died out, nothing ate the cats, excepting crabs and Chinese, but there were few Chinamen in those parts.

"Desmond, I could have left it in the swamp. Too late now."

"Oh, please Meester Rut, oh please! Do not do dis!"

But there was no turning Rut around. He threw the cat across the back of the golf cart and drove to the DNR office. No Callahan, Another officer at the desk.

"What in the hell happened to you?" the warden asked when Rut walked through the door."

"I got jumped by a panther," Rut said.

The warden smirked. "Now tell me what really happened."

"Get your sorry ass outside," Rut said.

The warden gave him the fish-eye but once outside he was clearly astounded. "Jesus H. Christ! I've never seen anything like this!"

"Me neither," Rut said.

"You shoot it?"

"I must have, but I really can't remember."

"You got some ID on you?"

Rut fished his driver's license out of his wallet, passed it over.

The warden read the particulars, passed it back. He keyed the radio mike clipped to his collar. "Backup at Marine Division, backup." The radio squawked back, but Rut couldn't make out the words.

"Mr. Elliott," the warden said, "you are under arrest."

Chapter Sixteen

Jailbirds and Daddies

Callahan put the cuffs on him, hands behind his back. She answered the call for backup, pushed him up against the fender of her truck. In this Age of Sexual Awareness, protocol insists female officers pat down female prisoners and must always be present when females are arrested, fewer bogus lawsuits that way. But when the warden went to pat Rut down, Callahan said, "I got this Mike."

There was love in her fingers as she ran her hands across his pockets and down the insides of both his legs. But Lordy she was pissed. She put her lips an inch from his ear and hissed. "Keep your freaking mouth shut and I will do what I can to get you out of this crack."

He nodded, "Yass'um."

"You got a lawyer?"

"No ma'am."

"You'd better get one." Then she whispered, "This baby doesn't need a jailbird for a daddy."

Washed in the Blood

"What?"

Callahan cinched the cuffs another click, cinched them till they hurt. "If it's a boy, we'll call him Tailgate."

The cat went on ice and up to Columbia for a post-mortem. Rut went to the Beaufort County Jail. He'd been there before. They took his belt and his billfold, his fingerprints and his picture. They always seem to arrest a man on a Friday afternoon, so he would have to wait till Monday to get a judge to set bond, Tuesday if the judge was busy as they generally were after a rowdy weekend in Beaufort County. The Feds had de-listed the Eastern Panther after declaring it extinct but the state never got around to it so we was charged with violating the South Carolina Endangered Species Act, which specifically prohibited "harassing, taking or possessing" any listed animal, or any part thereof, of which the Eastern Panther, *Puma concolor*, was one. Up to five years in prison, a ten-thousand-dollar fine and lifetime suspension of hunting and fishing privileges.

They allowed him one phone call. Instead of a lawyer, he called Mudbank Mammy's, left a message for Jen: "Hey honey please feed my chickens till Tuesday. You can keep the eggs."

No matter what jailhouse food tastes like, it's turkey, the cheapest meat they can get. An apple and a turkey bologna sandwich for supper, scrambled powdered eggs, white bread toast with grape jelly with no butter, and turkey bacon for breakfast.

He went before the judge just before noon on Monday. Callahan was not there, just the warden who had arrested him and a thin young man in government khakis, no pistol and a name tag that read "Drinkwater." It was the son-of-a-bitch who sent Rut those emails.

Drinkwater shook his hand. "Nice to finally meet you, Mr. Elliott."

"Sorry for my attire," said Rut, who was wearing an orange jumpsuit. The jail nurse had dressed his scratches but he hadn't showered in days. He was pretty ripe.

"I think there has been a terrible mistake."

"There Goddamn-sure has," Rut replied.

A burly, bald-headed bailiff stood at the door of the judge's chamber. He wore a big billy stick and a bigger revolver. Retired deputy, Rut reckoned, picking up a little extra money doing court duty. "You can't talk like that in here!" he hollered.

The door swung open and the judge breezed into the room, his robe unbuttoned and fapping in his wake. "Court's in session, everybody rise!"

They were all standing anyway.

The judge sat down. They did too.

The judge shuffled some papers, put on his reading glasses. "We're here this morning to accept a plea and to set bail in the matter of the state versus William Rutledge Elliott for violation …"

Warden Mike interrupted. "Your Honor, the state requests the charges be dropped."

The judge put the papers down, peered at the warden over his reading glasses. "It appears the defendant here has taken an

Washed in the Blood

endangered species, possessed an endangered species and has admitted to both. And you wish the charges dismissed?"

It was Drinkwater's turn. "Yes, Your Honor, we are awaiting results from the DNA lab but preliminary investigation by state biologists found there were few parasites in the intestines of the animal and there were unusual scuffing marks on the pads of all four paws consistent with walking on concrete. There is also an issue with the animal's color. There has never been a melanistic cat scientifically documented in the population of either the Western or Eastern subspecies of *Puma concolor*. It is the department's conclusion Mr. Elliott defended himself from an attack by an escaped exotic pet, which he had every right to do."

The judge leaned back in his chair, shook his head. "Mr. Drinkwater, I have been a lawyer my entire life, spent 15 years on the bench as a circuit court judge. I must admit I have never heard of anything like this."

Drinkwater went on. "Me neither, Your Honor. But it is the agency's opinion further prosecution would not stand legal scrutiny. Mr. Elliott has suffered injury and has been grossly inconvenienced. He may have grounds for a countersuit in a civil matter. If Mr. Elliott agrees to not pursue the matter further, I recommend dismissal."

The judge looked at Rut. "Mr. Elliott, do you agree with conditions?"

It galled Rut's gizzard to agree. But he wanted the hell out of that jail before they snooped around his garden and turned up what was left of his reefer crop. "Yes, Your Honor, I agree,"

The judge shrugged. "Very well, I'll have the clerk prepare the paperwork. You will be released upon your execution of the documents." His gavel came down, *whack*. "Case dismissed!"

"One other thing, Your Honor. My boat's at the Port Royal Marina. Is there any way I could hook a ride back there?"

The judge glared. "The court in not involved in the taxi business, Mr. Elliott."

"Your Honor, the law brought me here, the least it could do is take me back."

"One more word, Mr. Elliott, and I will find you in contempt of court."

Contempt of Court, thirty days, no jury trial, thirty more days of turkey bologna. Rut had nothing but contempt for this court but he counted his blessings and kept mum.

"I believe I can arrange that, Your Honor," Warden Mike said.

Rut sat naked on the edge of his bed, his feet on the cool pine floor boards. First cold snap of October now, no need for the window unit. All the reefer was cut, cleaned, bagged and put away, 10 grand easy, taxes and chump change for another year. The river breeze coursed over his body and it felt good.

Ten days later, he still hurt bad way down deep in muscle and bone. Callahan was naked beside him, cleaning his hurts with peroxide and later daubing with Neosporin ointment. She worked his shoulder with strong long fingers, fiddle paying fingers. Her belly was like a ripe melon and her sweet navel stuck out like the end of a big man's little finger.

"That thing swatted you good," she said.

"What thing," he replied. "It don't exist."

Her hands were working his whiplash neck at the time. She

reached up and grabbed a handful of hair at the base of his skull, rolled his head back, pulled his lips to hers. "Shut the hell up," she said.

He did.